Zephan and the Vision

Chris Wright

Zephan and the Vision

Chris Wright

First published in the United States of America
by Lighthouse Christian Publishing © Chris Wright 2007

This revised edition © Chris Wright 2012

ISBN 13: 978-0-952-5956-9-4

PUBLISHED BY
WHITE TREE PUBLISHING
28 FALLODON WAY
BRISTOL BS9 4HX
UNITED KINGDOM

For David, Eva, and Alexander

Books by Chris Wright for young readers
See back pages for more details

Agathos, The Rocky Island, and Other Stories

Mary Jones and Her Bible – An Adventure Book

Pilgrim's Progress – An Adventure Book

Pilgrim's Progress – Special Edition

Zephan and the Vision

INTRODUCTION

This book is an allegory – a story with a hidden meaning. Probably the most famous Christian allegory ever is *The Pilgrim's Progress* written by John Bunyan in 1678. In it, a man called Christian travels through life to the Celestial City, meeting all sorts of people along the way. Some of these people help him, but most of them try to stop him completing his journey. One of my favourite episodes is where Christian decides to take what he thinks is an easier path, is caught by Giant Despair, and is imprisoned in Doubting Castle. John Bunyan uses *The Pilgrim's Progress* to show us that in our Christian lives we face all sorts of difficulties and temptations on our way to Heaven, and he makes these difficulties and temptations appear as a mixed bag of people.

John Bunyan wrote other allegories, including *The Holy War*. I have included some ideas from *The Holy War* in this book, because I feel the story is worth hearing today, although in the original it is a very long and complicated read. However, the angels and their exploits, as well as the characters of Max and Nadia, are from my own imagination.

The narrator here is an angel called Zephan. A lot of nonsense is written about angels, so to repeat what Zephan says in this book, "I want to get one thing straight – we're not make-believe figures like fairies and pixies!" And he's right. The Bible tells us that the Lord God created angels to do his work. We must not pray to angels or tell them what to do – the Lord God gives them their instructions. Angels are mentioned over three hundred and fifty times in the Bible: from Genesis to Revelation – in thirty-seven books in total. If you want to know more about angels, read your Bible, not New Ages sites on the internet and far-fetched magazines!

We don't know what angels are made from, or how they can travel long distances, but they are obviously very different from us. Some people think that the spiritual world is like a parallel world mixed with ours, in which case angels don't need to travel very far. It's an interesting possibility, but no more than that. Humans, of course, are part of the Earth's carbon-based creation, sharing very similar DNA to animals. The Creator God made the first person from what the Bible calls "dust" or "dirt" – the basic building blocks of life – otherwise we would not be able to eat Earth's food. The Bible tells us that the first people differed from the animals because God gave them souls, so their descendants – like you and like me – can know and love the Lord God and live with him in Heaven forever. But as we see here, the Lord God has a dangerous enemy.

In *The Holy War* John Bunyan shows sin entering the innocent town of Mansoul, rather than repeating the Genesis account of Adam and Eve in the Garden of Eden. This might seem a strange mistake from someone who knew his Bible so well, but I believe Bunyan was showing how people gave in to temptation at the beginning, and give in to it now. Many of the "people" living in Bunyan's Mansoul are exactly like parts of me, and probably you, so the citizens may well be just two people – Adam and Eve. Anyway, in this story I have gone with Bunyan by having Mansoul full of people, because I think this makes a very exciting and memorable picture – an allegory – of what is called "The Fall". However, unlike *The Holy War*, the story told here quickly moves on to battles between God and God's enemy the devil (Diabolus) in the present day.

The creatures living around the castles are more like our thoughts and temptations than real people, or sometimes they are things that other people say, but not everything in my allegory stands for something else. For instance the castle windows, roofs, trumpets, rocks, woods, the cave and so on are props, necessary for telling the story and nothing more. I hope I have told the story simply enough without anyone feeling the need to spend time looking for too many hidden meanings along the way!

An excellent book is *Angels* by Dr. Billy Graham, that has sold several million copies. I have tried to follow the Bible teaching about angels, but there have obviously been times when I needed to use some writer's licence to help the story along. This is an allegory, not a true account, trying to show how much the Lord God loves us. There isn't really a town of Mansoul, or someone called The Magnificent Great-Hopes, and yet … and yet in a way there is. And that's the whole point of this allegory!

Chris Wright
Bristol

CHAPTER 1

A Crimson Sky

There we were, two ordinary angels sitting on a rock under a drelgo tree, caring for the planet Eltor. And that's when the problems started. Of course, as angels we should always have one eye open for danger, but on that hot day I have to admit that danger was far from our minds.

You won't have heard of Eltor – it's in a galaxy far, far away, as they say. The twin red suns of Caspar were already soaring high above the orange sand, glaring down from a fiery, crimson sky. Red leaves of the drelgo tree gave shelter to the tiny creatures running all around us.

I moved my feet to allow a gisko to carry a dried leaf to line her nest for the coming winter. Winter is when the twin suns of Caspar never rise above the horizon, and tornados ravage Eltor, blasting the rocks and reshaping the landscape.

"Do you know that there's a planet where the sky is blue?" I asked Talora, my thoughts far away. By the way, my name is Zephan. Zephan means "Treasured by God". Please don't think the name gives me special privileges – God treasures all his angels equally, although he gives some angels much more responsible work than others. Talora and I were looking after Eltor, which was hardly a major appointment compared to the mission of the Lord God's warrior angels – and it's good that we'll be meeting them later. Even so, we took our work seriously.

Maybe you're wondering how old we are. Angels aren't humans. Well, I imagine everyone knows that. We're spirit beings, usually invisible to people and animals. We don't marry or have children. No men, no women, boys or girls. It's just that we sometimes *look* like people when we appear on Earth. If we were to appear to you now, you'd almost certainly see us as young people – with Talora as the girl and me as the boy. So I'll call Talora "she" if it helps.

How old are we? Talora might not like it if I told you, but here's a clue: all angels are old – as old as creation itself. Talora's name means – now please don't smile – "Morning Dew". No, it's not really funny. It's just that we've never seen dew here on Eltor – not in the morning, or at any other time of the day. The twin suns see to that. At this time, I don't think Talora had seen morning dew anywhere, but it's a great name.

"Do you know that there's a planet where the sky is blue?" I had to repeat the question, because Talora didn't seem to be listening.

She looked at me, grinned politely and laughed. "I heard you." Then, "I've been wondering how any sky can be blue," she said, adding rather obviously that the twin suns of Eltor made everything red – or orange.

I was right, Talora probably never had seen dew. You need a blue sky to get dew. "And the sea is blue," I added, trying to recall a couple of visits to the planet called Earth.

"I've heard about Earth." Talora gazed up into the scorching sky. "It's where there's nothing but trouble nowadays. Not that I've ever been there. And I still don't remember what blue is." She sighed softly. "We've been on Eltor a long time."

I thought for a moment, and then it came to me. I looked

closely at Talora. "My eyes. See? They're blue."

Talora studied them, and then laughed. "Sky and sea the colour of your eyes? Go on, Zephan, pull the other wing."

"And most of the plants are green."

"Green?"

"The colour of *your* eyes. And there are flowers of all sorts of colours."

"Red?" Talora asked, with a hint of teasing in her voice.

Yes, angels do occasionally tease each other. Well, some do. Not the major angels. Especially not archangels. Not even cherubim and seraphim, and certainly not the warrior angels. But ordinary ones like us do from time to time. It helps pass the day, but we never argue about things. Not very often, and never seriously.

I told her, "I've seen flowers that are blue, yellow, purple. Even pink."

Talora became quiet as she looked up into the sky. "I can believe it," she admitted. "Everyone knows the Creator made millions of suns and planets in the Universe."

I moved my feet again to let the furry gisko scuttle past with yet another leaf. Maybe the creature knew the coming winter would be even more harsh than usual. "I only went there for a short time. Twice," I added, casually. It wouldn't do to boast about travel to faraway places.

"Tell me, Zephan, was that before there were people?"

"The first time was definitely before the Creator made people. I saw some giant creatures."

"How giant?"

I couldn't remember them all that clearly. After all, for the past few thousand years all we'd seen were teeny little things like giskos, so most of the creatures on Earth would seem large in comparison. I pointed up at the drelgo tree that we were using for shade. "Giant enough to make this tree seem like a small bush."

"That *is* big," Talora agreed. "Are the people afraid of them?"

"The biggest creatures died out a long time ago. There are mostly smaller animals now. People keep some of the very small ones as pets."

"Pets?"

"They're tame. They don't hurt people, and people don't hurt them."

"These giskos are tame, Zephan, but I wouldn't want to keep one." Talora shivered. "They're much too wriggly."

"Well, that's what people do," I told her. "They have pet animals called cats, dogs and rabbits, and things like that."

"I've never seen people," Talora said wistfully.

"I have, the second time I went to Earth. An angel took me on a flying visit."

Talora got the joke, and smiled dutifully. "What did you see?"

"I was only there for an afternoon. The people looked a bit like us – except they didn't have wings."

"No *wings*?"

So that came as a surprise. "And many of them don't even bother about the Creator."

Talora looked at me in amazement. "If it was me I would send a huge comet." She frowned. "Or an asteroid. The Lord God should smash the planet to pieces to punish everyone."

"The Creator loves his Earth. Especially his people." I moved my feet yet again. I was only repeating what I'd heard from other angels, but I knew it was true. "See that gisko? See how she loves her children?"

I watched Talora pull her white cloak around her wings and

shoulders as protection from the heat blasting through the leaves of the drelgo tree from the twin suns of Caspar. "I know about love," she said. "That's why the gisko is making a place to keep her children safe during the winter. It's no trouble for her to be fetching and carrying leaves all day long." Talora stopped and rubbed a few tears from her eyes.

I pulled a couple of brown leaves from the tree, and dropped them on the ground for the gisko to find. "You look sad."

"I *am* sad," Talora said. "All this talk of bad things on the planet Earth. The spiritual world is all I've ever wanted."

That made me laugh, but not in an unkind way. To tell you the truth, I've always preferred the spiritual world to the physical one. Did I just say something about telling the truth? As if God's angels can do anything else! I've already mentioned we're not like people. We chose to follow the Lord God at creation, and now we have no alternative to be anything but honest and obedient. Please don't worry. It's how we are – and it's how we want to be.

You, of course, are different. You can choose to do good things and you can choose to do wrong things. Almost certainly you find yourself doing both. You can ask God to forgive you, or you can tell yourself that it doesn't matter what you do. It's up to you, and it's what we call free will.

Of course, there are angels who are bad. Not just bad. Evil and deceitful. We call them shadow angels – and they're guaranteed to spoil anything if you let them. And we're meeting *them* later.

"I often wonder how time works," Talora continued. "There only seems to be such a thing as time when we're here on Eltor. When we're around the throne of God we are – well, we're just there."

I agreed. "It's funny to think of eternity when all we can see are the twin suns going round every day."

"*Zephan and Talora, I know your thoughts.*" The gentle voice we loved so much floated through the heat. "*You work hard for me here, but there is much you do not understand.*"

I need hardly say we'd fallen to our knees.

CHAPTER 2

Questions

Talora was the first to speak. "O Lord God," she said, "we praise you and worship you now."

"*Do you want to do some other work?*"

"Here on Eltor there is much work to do." Talora spoke in a respectful way. She pointed to me. "Zephan and I enjoy working together. I would like to stay with him."

I found myself suddenly wondering if … No, surely the Lord God hadn't heard Talora's questions about Earth; hadn't understood her interest in the planet as a wish to actually *go* there. That place was full of danger – even for angels.

I remember noticing how the air of Eltor shimmered as the loving voice of the Creator rang out over the orange sand. Even the gisko paused in her task of preparing for winter. The voice seemed to give her more comfort than a nest of the finest dried leaves.

"Do you want us to *fight* for you on earth?" I asked after a long silence, and I think I sounded anxious. Fighting wasn't exactly what I had in mind. "I mean, I know a *bit* about the place, but …" I stopped. My nervousness made me sound foolish. Of course, I couldn't say I knew a *lot* about the Earth if I didn't. I don't mean that I could have pretended I knew, but chose not to. It's just that we angels *can't* pretend. I hope you're starting to see how different angels are from people. And I don't just mean wings.

There was a long silence before the Lord God spoke again.

The little gisko discovered the leaves I'd pulled from the drelgo tree.

"Do you think you are too inexperienced to fight against my enemy?" the Creator continued at last.

I suddenly felt bolder. "I know we're not like your powerful warrior angels, but angels like us might be able to get into the enemy's camp unnoticed. Sometimes. Perhaps." I knew my boldness was deserting me, even though what I said was true.

"What do you know about people?"

I felt tongue-tied, but I had to answer. I lifted my arms to the sky. "Somewhere out there you've made a very special creation. They're called men, women, children."

"What else?"

I knew much more than that, but I wasn't going to show off. Compared to the Creator God I knew almost nothing. "They live in a world rather like this, but with only one sun."

"That is good. And?"

"They can't understand the invisible side of creation, for they are strangely made."

"Strangely made?"

I could sense the Lord God smiling as he spoke. "I mean they're not like angels," I replied. It wasn't for me to question the Creator's ways. Then I remembered something else. "They can do something angels cannot do – they can call you Father."

"Indeed they can, Zephan. And you, Talora, do you know why I am sad for the people of Earth?"

"Because they have turned away from you, and followed Diabolus your enemy?" She made her reply sound like a question.

"That is also a good answer," the Creator replied softly and tenderly. *"A wise one, Talora."*

"There's still much I need to learn," Talora admitted. "I

mean, how can people on Earth turn away from you when you love them much, much more than this little gisko loves her young?”

“Oh, Talora, I love people even more than you can imagine.”

Silence fell over Eltor, and we stayed on our knees.

“You have served me well here,” the Creator said eventually. *“And now I want you to serve me on Earth.”*

“If that is your will,” I replied. I hope I made the point clear just now, when I said angels are obedient. We get great pleasure in obeying the Lord God. I guess I could say we’re programed to be like that. But I don’t want anyone to feel troubled on our behalf. It simply isn’t a problem.

“O Lord God, we will serve you anywhere,” Talora added, as though not giving it a second thought, which is how it should be.

“There is much danger there,” the Creator warned.

Talora sounded insistent. “We will serve you in *any* danger.”

“Then you must both see for yourselves how treacherous my enemy Diabolus can be. The planet Earth is his battleground. The enemy wants to spoil and destroy all that is good. But my plan is to search for people and rescue them.”

Talora spoke first, but now sounded hesitant. “We’re excited that you want us to go to Earth, but … but we wouldn’t know what to do when we got there. Will you send someone to teach us?”

I’m not sure I felt over-excited by the prospect of danger. After all, I knew more about the shadow angels than Talora did. The twin suns had now reached their highest point in the sky, and the air was too hot. I looked around, but stayed kneeling. Most of the small creatures had scampered for the shelter of their burrows beneath the drelgo trees. I caught sight of the last one scurrying out of sight. Perhaps it had stayed to keep an inquisitive eye on us.

"Zephan and Talora, lie down in the shade of that large rock and I will show you a vision. It is a picture of the battles I have fought on Earth since I first made people. You can walk around inside the vision and see many things. But you must remember it is a record of the past, so you will not be able to change anything."

"And when we've seen it?" I asked, wondering what was ahead for us both.

"Then you will be ready to go to Earth to take part in my battles."

"I think I see," I said, and of course I did think it at the time. As I said, we can only tell the truth. The Lord God was about to show us how it all went wrong for the human race, but it sounded as though he was going to let us see it as a sort of picture. Well, that seemed like a good idea.

Men? Women? Children? What is it really like to be a person? That, of course, is something angels can never know. The Lord God created angels and people, but to be an angel is not to be a human. Humans know so little about the Creator, whereas we angels can regularly gather round his throne and see him with our eyes.

"Come on, Talora, we have to lie down by that rock." I took hold of her arm. "The Lord God has said so."

"Oh, Zephan," Talora whispered uneasily, "why did I feel so excited a moment ago? How do people live and think? I've no idea what to do when we get to Earth."

"That's why we're going to see the vision, so we can learn before we go."

Neither of us spoke again.

CHAPTER 3

The Vision

The planet Eltor became strangely dark as we lay down. We felt ourselves going back, back to a distant past.

Suddenly I felt a stirring in the hot sand. A massive wall and buildings sprang up in front of us. A soft change of colour spread over the red sky until it became blue, the colour of my eyes. A noise filled the air.

I raised my head. People – not angels – hurried backwards and forwards in and out of a gateway to a busy town. Over the gateway I could see a large sign, but it was too far away to read. I pulled Talora to her feet. No one stopped to ask us what we were doing.

"You're right," Talora said quietly. "People do look very much like us."

I want to get one thing straight – we're not make-believe figures like fairies and pixies! The Creator God made us, which is why we serve and worship him – why we were here now. Actually, I want to get another thing straight – you don't become an angel when you die. One day you'll get a new body in Heaven, but you'll still be a person. I hope that's clear.

I looked around in excitement. Everything seemed so touchable. It was hard to understand that this was a vision of the past.

"I'm sure we're invisible," Talora said as we walked forward slowly. "No one's looking at us."

Well, that was a relief. Imagine what it's like for two angels like us suddenly arriving on Earth from Eltor. I mean, what would people make of us if they could see our wings? No wonder angels choose to be invisible most of the time. Anyway, we couldn't have dressed like these people for disguise, even if we'd wanted to. Their clothes wouldn't go round our wings – although I had a feeling our wings may not always be visible, even when the rest of us can be seen.

To you, this vision would be a bit like watching a film, but not exactly. Think of it like watching a 3D film and getting inside it at the same time – being able to walk around and touch things, but not being able to change anything. Of course, we were simply onlookers on something that happened long ago, no matter how real everything appeared. So I suppose even if they could see us, the people wouldn't be able to talk to us. Even so – and this might sound silly – I felt a lot safer being invisible.

As we got closer to the town walls, we stopped. The large sign over the gateway told us we were entering Mansoul.

CHAPTER 4

Inside the Town

"Mansoul?" Talora asked. "What is Mansoul, Zephan?"

"It looks like a fortified town," I said. "The Lord God must have built it for his people." I don't think I was telling Talora something she couldn't have worked out for herself, because the high walls and the name over the gateway were easy enough to see. I think she was nervous. Well, so was I.

"It looks good," Talora said, frowning. "If the Creator's own people live here, where's the problem?"

The problem, of course, was that the Lord God had an enemy, although I have to admit the town walls looked strong enough to keep anyone out. The massive wooden gates in the wall had no gaps. We could see a large ear carved into the stonework on a tower above the gateway. A man stood on top with what looked like a huge trumpet in his hands, but he held it to his ear, not his mouth. He turned it slowly to the left and right, then back again, as though straining to pick up the slightest sound. But what was he listening for?

Talora took hold of my hand. "This must be the Ear Gate. Do you think the man will let us in if we ask?"

I shook my head. "This is all happening in the past. We're not able to talk to anyone."

"Then I'm going to fly over the wall and see what's inside

the town." Talora sounded really wound up. "And because this is a vision, no one can stop me."

Call me over-cautious, but I can't say I shared Talora's enthusiasm. I wanted to check everything first, just to make sure we were really safe. "Let's walk all the way round before going in."

Talora agreed – reluctantly. We made our way past a group of men and women talking outside the high walls. None of them took any notice of us as we walked past, and I was glad about that. It's just that I still had this feeling that if people saw us, they might somehow be able to cause problems. All right, it was silly, but that's how I felt.

"Another gate," Talora announced after a few minutes' walking. "I can see an eye carved in the stone over this one."

High on the wall a man stood with a large telescope in his hands, scanning the horizon, backwards and forwards.

"The Eye Gate," I guessed. This was hardly brilliant, but you find yourself saying things like that when you're jumpy. "Come on, let's see if there are any more gates."

We found people unloading a large wagon of fresh food outside the next gate. Others helped carry it through the gate into the town.

"The Mouth Gate." It was Talora's turn to say the obvious, as she pointed up at a carved stone showing an open mouth. "And look how fresh the food is."

It may seem strange that angels, who don't generally need to eat, should be able to judge the quality of food. But this delivery would make anyone's mouth water. I noticed Talora licking her lips.

We continued our walk, and must have gone more than half way round the town when we heard a strange rushing sound. The noise kept stopping for a few seconds before continuing.

"Quickly," Talora said, pulling me on. "It must be another gate."

I held back. The sound was scary. "So what is it?"

We saw it before either of us could guess – a gate with the carving of a nose above it.

I couldn't help making a joke. "Let's hope we're not around when they blow it!"

Talora was too absorbed by what she saw to even hear me. The guardian had the gate only slightly open, held by a secure chain. As we watched, we saw that no one could get in through the gap without his permission. A smell of fresh flowers and cooking filled the air. Some of the people stood on the town wall above the gate and breathed in deeply, smiling at the heady scent.

"We'll be back where we started soon," I said.

"Come on, Zephan, this must be the last gate." Talora was going much too quickly for my liking. She turned round. "Do keep up."

The gate was tall and narrow. "One more guess," I offered.

Talora shook her shoulders, and her wings fluttered. "No idea."

We walked forward slowly. The tall, thin gate had a finger carved into the stone above it. Touch Gate, the sign said. A woman carrying a large bundle of wood on her back stopped outside. The gate moved open slightly. The guardian stood in front of her, prodding the bundle.

"Pass in safety," he told her. "You present no danger to the town."

The woman nodded, and disappeared into a maze of narrow streets. The gate closed, blocking our view.

"Well, Zephan, are we going in or not?" Talora asked impatiently.

"It's closed," I told her. "The guard can't see us, so he's not going to open it."

Talora rustled her wings gently. "Then we'll fly over the wall. It's time we explored inside." And before I could say anything, she was off the ground and soaring over the town walls.

Our wings look quite small and neat when folded, in the way that a seagull's wings look when it's resting. But, like a gull, when we spread our wings they're long and extremely powerful. I imagine you're thinking that if you were an angel you'd spend your time flying here, there and everywhere. But I can assure you the novelty soon wears off. Unless we're making a long journey, most of the angels I know prefer to walk. Of course, sometimes it's easier to fly, especially when we're in a hurry or need to get over high walls. And flying was the only sensible way for us to get into the town of Mansoul – probably the only way. A few seconds later we landed unseen in one of the streets.

Inside the town everything felt safe. Let me explain what I mean by safe. Perhaps you've visited an ancient town while on holiday, and started down a dark, narrow passageway. Plaster peeling off the walls, dirty windows, deep shadows. Your heart beats faster and you decide it's time to turn back, just in case something or someone unpleasant is round the corner. Mansoul wasn't like that. It was the cleanest, brightest town anyone ever saw. Everything looked recently built, perfect in every detail.

We sat close to a tall tree that bore some sort of fruit. It all seemed familiar and I wondered why. Certainly this was nothing like the drelgo trees on Eltor. I can't remember the exact words, but a sign hanging from a low branch said something like, *This is the Tree of Knowledge of Good and Evil. Do not eat the Fruit.* I don't think there were any other regulations or laws in the town. The people obviously had no wish to do anything other than treat each other fairly and honestly – and remember their Creator. In other words, everything was just right. A bit like Heaven.

In the centre of the town we discovered a castle, with a strong tower in the middle. I asked Talora to sit with me on the green outside the castle walls, so we could watch the comings and goings of the people.

"War in Heaven, war on Earth," I said quietly, still anxious that we might be overheard, although deep down I knew it was impossible in this vision.

Talora nodded. "It all seems so peaceful. When are we going to understand what happened here long ago?"

Trouble was coming, I knew it for sure, and I wondered what it would be like for us, standing as spectators in the middle of a violent battle. I wanted to be back on Eltor. Or, even better, around the throne of the Creator God singing praises with millions of other angels. Millions of angels? If you were able to travel through the Universe like us, you might think it's easy to say "millions" and have a real understanding of … what, how big a million is? More likely, you'd know just how small a number it is. Billions. Billions of miles, billions of stars, billions of planets. Last time I was in Heaven I didn't count how many angels were gathered round the throne singing, but I reckon I should be saying millions and millions. All of us ready to work for the Lord God. I remember how Talora had often stood with me with me in Heaven in adoration of our Creator.

Before you ask, there's no way I can explain what sort of music we have in Heaven. Even if I could sing it for you, you wouldn't be able to join in – because you're not ready for it yet. Nor could you play it on your musical instruments, although you sometimes think you get close. It's a very different sort of music. It's … well, it's the music of Heaven – and I can't put it any better than that. But I can promise that you'd think it was beautiful.

We sat on the green by the castle for much of the afternoon, chatting about what we'd already seen in the town of Mansoul. Wild flowers grew all around us, the first flowers of various colours that Talora said she'd ever seen. And she got really excited by their different scents.

Suddenly we heard a buzz of excitement, and I was astonished to see the Lord God coming into the town. I know we were seeing a picture of the past, but even so, we fell on our knees as the people rushed up to him to thank him for the love and care he showed. This was a town with no sickness or death. No wonder everyone seemed happy.

The people led the Lord God into the strong tower in the centre of the castle. Talora went with me, eager to see what was inside – a stunning throne covered in gold and precious stones, surely made specially for the Creator. When he spoke, a feeling of love and peace flooded every corner of the room. The people let out a wonderful cry of praise, almost as wonderful as the praise of the angels around the throne in Heaven. I have to say I was impressed, for until then I thought angels won hands-down when it came to praising.

And then the Lord God had gone, as suddenly as he'd come.

CHAPTER 5

Diabolus

Outside the town, green fields and tall trees stretched into the distance – and not a drelgo tree in sight. How different everything was from the red and orange sands of Eltor. I have to admit I grew restless and kept wondering what was out there. We'd seen most of the town, and I wanted to explore the countryside. I felt drawn by a strange-looking hill that had a heavy shadow over it. On top of the hill grew a forest of withered trees, and I decided to take a closer look.

As we flew almost silently, Talora, who was following, grabbed hold of my ankle. "Don't go down, Zephan," she shouted in alarm.

I stopped, hovering in the air, looking to see where Talora was pointing. There, at the foot of the hill, within sight of the town, I saw the Lord God's enemy. I've already mentioned him. He's the one who hates the Creator and all he's made. This enemy probably hated the town of Mansoul more than anything else in the Universe.

"I'm sure the people of Mansoul don't know he's here," I said in a whisper, and shuddered. Maybe we'd been too sheltered on Eltor. "He's Diabolus, the devil who was once one of God's angels. I suppose we should have expected to find him here."

"It's all *his* fault there's trouble," Talora complained, as we continued to soar above the hill. "Why did he decide to go against the Lord God?"

"What's this, a riddle?"

"No, Zephan, it's a sensible question."

I decided it was indeed a sensible question, and I shrugged – which is something angels can only do with difficulty while flying. "I've heard he wanted to be as great as God himself."

Talora shook her head. "As great as the Lord God, the Creator of the Universe?"

I said nothing. How could any angel be so foolish as to think such a thing possible? Diabolus, like all the angels, was created. Not created evil, but created with a free choice. And he rebelled against the Lord God. Some angels chose to go with him – not just a few angels, but many, many of them. The war in Heaven was on the unseen side of the Lord God's creation, but it was so dreadful that it spilled over onto the visible side.

Mansoul looked so perfect in this vision, but I knew this was about to change. Soon there would be only one place worse than the planet Earth, and that was the terrible kingdom of God's enemy.

"There are shadow angels with him." Talora closed her eyes and kept them closed. "Imagine, Zephan, imagine being a shadow angel living in the kingdom of darkness, shut out from the sight of the Lord God – never able to see his face again. Never able to gather round his throne and sing his praises. I can't start to think what it must be like." Talora opened her eyes again, which was just as well, as she was losing height rapidly.

"Cheer up," I said, staying with her. "We know the war on earth will end in victory for the Lord God."

"Shouldn't we warn the people that Diabolus is hiding below the hill?" Talora asked in panic.

"This is just a vision," I reminded her. "Everything we're seeing here happened a long time ago. All we can do is watch and learn. Let's go down."

CHAPTER 6

An Evil Plan

As we swooped over the encampment, thousands of the followers of Diabolus, the shadow angels, stood below the hill and began to cheer loudly. We pulled back in fright and hovered on a rising current of warm air to listen.

Diabolus got to his feet in the centre of the gathering and rubbed his hands together. "The town will be mine," he shouted, and the shadow angels cheered again. "We will smash down the work of the Creator and ..."

"We will build *your* statue there, O great and mighty prince," one of the shadow angels interrupted. "Long live Diabolus!"

We heard the cry repeated around the camp, until Diabolus was forced to call a halt to this devotion by his followers.

"Fools," he called. "Do you want everyone in the town of Mansoul to know we are so close? If they see or hear us, they will be ready to defend the gates."

I watched one of the shadow angels hold up a hand. "If it pleases your majesty, don't you think the people will be frightened by ...?"

"Yes?"

The shadow angel took a deep breath. "What I mean is, because of your face ..."

"Yes?"

"It is a great and noble face, of course – to us – but the people may not …"

Diabolus stamped in rage. "I am entering Mansoul as a conqueror, not as a guest."

Another shadow angel interrupted him. "Are you sure you need us with you?"

Diabolus stamped on the ground again, and we could hear the sound rumble through the hill. "You all agreed to come on this mission. You all agreed that the Creator has treated us badly. Is there not a place for us in Heaven? Is it right for the Creator to have all the power?"

The shadow angels set up such a roar of approval that Talora gripped me tightly, trapping one of my wings with her arm. For a moment I thought I was going to crash, but I recovered as soon as she let go. "I think it's time we went," she said urgently.

"I'm staying," I told her. "I want to see what happens next."

"Come," Diabolus shouted to his troops. "We will march into the town."

"Let me shoot the keeper of the Ear Gate," one of the shadow angels suggested. "I have a powerful bow. He will not be prepared for such an attack."

"You speak well." Diabolus sounded calmer now. "We will all go to the town, and I shall wear a helmet and cloak so that neither my face …" He glared at the shadow angel who had spoken first. "So that neither my *face* nor my dark armour can be seen." He turned to a shadow angel who held a trumpet. "When we get to the gate, announce my presence."

Talora struck out strongly with her wings and rose swiftly into the air.

"Where are you going?" I called, working hard to keep up.

"To warn the people, of course. They are ..." Talora stopped. "Oh, Zephan, I keep forgetting." She looked down at the army of shadow angels as they prepared to destroy the town of Mansoul. "Is there nothing we can do to help the people?"

"Nothing," I told her. "Absolutely nothing."

CHAPTER 7

Attack!

Diabolus and his army of shadow angels reached the outside of the town quickly, and hid in the shelter of some leafy trees below the high walls.

"We will be safe here," we heard Diabolus explain to the shadow angels. "The Keeper of the Ear Gate has not taken notice of us yet." He called to his trumpeter. "Go forward and announce my presence."

The Ear Gate was tightly closed, but when the trumpet sounded the people of Mansoul rushed to the walls.

"Where's Captain Resistance?" they called to each other when they saw Diabolus and his army below. "Find Captain Resistance at once!"

A man in lightweight silver armour stepped forward to cheers from the crowd. I nudged Talora. "If that's Captain Resistance, there's going to be trouble for Mansoul."

Talora held my hand as we hovered, careful not to let our wings clash. "What is he going to do?"

"Not much. You know how the giskos run all round us on Eltor? They're tame. They've never seen an enemy, so they wouldn't be prepared if one came."

"So?"

"It's the same here. Did you see any soldiers in the town

when we explored it?"

"No."

"There aren't any. That man in thin armour is the only person in Mansoul who can fight for them."

I noticed that Diabolus was careful to keep his head low, probably afraid the people would be frightened by his face – as one of the shadow angels had already hinted. Diabolus spoke with such a clear and gentle voice that even his shadow angels looked at each other in surprise.

"People of the town of Mansoul, you will see that I am here, like yourselves, to serve the Lord G … The Lord G …" He stopped and cleared his throat, unable to use the name. "I am here to serve your great King," he continued. "I have come to help you."

"Help us?" Captain Resistance called in surprise. "We're all happy here. We have no need of help."

Diabolus went to tip his head back, realised his helmet was slipping, and held it firmly with one hand. "Surely you are aware that you are captives in this town," he shouted.

The people at the Ear Gate turned to each other. "What does he mean?" they asked.

"Let's hear what our visitor has to say," someone shouted to Captain Resistance. "He may have come to tell us something good."

Diabolus wasn't waiting for permission to proceed. "People of Mansoul, I am so very sorry for you. Of course, I know that the Lord G …, the King, is great and powerful, and everything he has told you is true, but he has not told you the *whole* truth."

"Go away!" someone in the crowd called, but I noticed it wasn't Captain Resistance. I was really worried about the captain. His armour looked too flimsy for battle. Not only that, he didn't even seem aware of the danger.

"You had better explain what you mean," Captain Resistance called down slowly. "You're certainly mistaken if you think the Great King has deceived us. We are free to live as we like, and we have chosen to live like this."

"Really?" Diabolus answered, and his voice now sounded much louder. "Do you *really* think you are free to do as you like?"

I noticed Diabolus was careful to keep his face towards the ground, and he drew his cloak even more tightly around his dark armour. "If you are as free as you say, are you free to pick the fruit from that tree by the castle?"

"The Tree of Knowledge?" Captain Resistance shook his head. "We cannot eat from that. The King has said we are not to."

"Then you are *not* free."

This seemed to get Captain Resistance thinking. "The Creator has made us, and we *are* free," he called down at last.

"Go on then," Diabolus shouted. "Pick the fruit and eat it. If you do that, you will be like the King. Can *he* not do as he chooses?"

"Of course he can," the captain replied angrily.

"You are right," Diabolus called to the people staring down at him from the top of the town walls. "He can. And are you the King's own people?"

"We are," everyone shouted back in agreement.

Diabolus nodded. "Then it is only fair that you should be free to do as *you* choose."

I watched with Talora as the people held a long discussion. We could hear some of them saying surely the King would be pleased that they were doing what was only right and sensible. Then, all of a sudden, they rushed off to pick the fruit.

Talora clenched her fists in frustration. "And we can do

nothing to stop them!"

We watched as Captain Resistance leaned over the wall to hear the visitor more clearly. Below the walls, one of the shadow angels drew back his bow from the shelter of a rock by the Ear Gate and took careful aim.

I flew up higher so I could see the tree where I'd sat with Talora earlier. Then I looked back at Captain Resistance. Just as a woman reached out to take the fruit from the Tree of Knowledge, the arrow found its mark. Captain Resistance fell from the town walls and landed at the feet of Diabolus. Dead. The woman passed the fruit to a man who was with her.

"Make way for Lord Innocence," someone by the wall shouted.

A man hurried forward and leaned over the fortifications, trying to see where Captain Resistance had fallen. I think he recognised Diabolus for who he really was, because he opened his mouth and began to shout the name. But before Lord Innocence could complete the warning, he too fell to his death, pierced by an arrow from the shadow angel's bow.

Far from being frightened by the two deaths, the people ran to join their friends in eating the forbidden fruit. I stayed where I was with Talora, flying slowly just above the walls. It wasn't long before the people returned for another look at Diabolus. He certainly seemed well pleased with himself.

"Ah, Mansoul," Diabolus shouted to the people leaning over the town walls. I nudged Talora and pointed out how tightly Diabolus still held his cloak around his dark armour. "You will see that I was indeed right in advising you to eat the fruit."

Diabolus was now sure of the crowd's attention, and I think everyone in the town was there to hear him. "Can you not see that you are now as great as the Lord G ..., as the Creator?"

"How so?" a young man asked.

"Because you are free to do anything you like."

"Where's Captain Resistance?" a woman shouted. She must have been at the Tree of Knowledge of Good and Evil when disaster struck, and missed seeing the captain being shot by the arrow. "And where's Lord Innocence?"

"Ah, yes," Diabolus called back. "How sorry I am that two of your leaders chose to end their lives so tragically, by jumping off the walls of your beautiful town. Unfortunately some people are unable to face the truth. It is, of course, the truth that I come here to tell you today."

"Truth? What sort of truth?" the young man called down. The way he asked his question sounded as though he was willing to listen to the answer. I mean, he didn't make it sound like a scornful retort.

Diabolus obviously sensed the same thing. "You have been prisoners of the Creator, and now ... now you are *free*," he called back, still keeping his cloak wrapped tightly.

Talora took a sharp intake of breath as the people of Mansoul looked at each other and smiled. Diabolus was saying what they obviously wanted to hear. The fruit must have tasted good, and now they thought they were like the King, able to make their own choices, even if it meant disobeying the Creator.

Diabolus called up again. "Mansoul, you are now a poor, defenceless town."

"What can we do?" a young woman shouted in alarm. It was a terrified cry for help.

"You need someone *strong* to defend you," Diabolus told her. "Be warned, when the Creator hears what you have done, he will invade Mansoul and carry you all away as prisoners."

The people shook their heads and began to discuss this anxiously. I touched down just inside the walls with Talora and we walked among the people, unseen, listening to their worried discussions.

"We want *you* to be our king," the young man called down at last to Diabolus.

"Yes, be our king," the cry went up from along the walls.

CHAPTER 8

A Warning

We watched in dismay as the large Ear Gate swung open and the people led Diabolus and his shadow angels up to the castle in the centre of Mansoul – seating him with honour on the throne where the Lord God had sat so recently. The atmosphere now felt very different. I could sense hatred filling the chamber, although the people obviously thought everything was fine. As soon as Diabolus had greeted them they left, returning to their own homes after an eventful day. And everyone seemed remarkably pleased with their new king.

"Be quick," Diabolus warned his shadow angels as they gathered round. "Make fast the town gates. We have work to do. There are some people in Mansoul who will not accept me."

"Tell us who they are," a shadow angel snarled.

We kept still, even though we knew Diabolus and his followers wouldn't be able to see us. It's the sort of thing anyone would do in this situation, especially ordinary angels like us.

"The Mayor of Mansoul is likely to make the most trouble," Diabolus explained. "His name is Understanding. He recognised me, and I think he has already guessed my plans for the town. But he is not alone."

"And who else will not worship you?" several shadow angels asked in unison.

"Conscience, the Keeper of the Law."

One of the shadow angels pushed his way through to the front and bowed before the throne. "Understanding is sound asleep in his house," he reported breathlessly.

Diabolus clapped his hands in pleasure. "Then you must be quick and build a high wall to trap him inside. Seal his door and windows with timber. I do not want the smallest ray of sunlight piercing Understanding's house. Do you understand?"

"You want us to turn his house into a prison?" a shadow angel asked.

Diabolus grinned, and it wasn't a nice sight. "Yes, a prison. Cover Understanding's windows as well as his door, and he will be my prisoner for ever."

"Your prisoner for ever, for ever, for ever," the shadow angels chanted.

Diabolus seemed overjoyed to hear them. "If we are able to keep Understanding in darkness long enough, he will become blind. I know things about people."

Understanding, the Mayor, stayed asleep while the shadow angels turned his house into a prison. But the Keeper of the Law, Conscience, was much more difficult to deal with. Diabolus said he was hiding somewhere in the town, and ordered his shadow angels to find him immediately.

That night they failed in their task, and the next morning Conscience stood in the market square and shouted so loudly to warn everyone about Diabolus, that Mansoul seemed to shake with an earthquake. Talora and I felt excited by this act of rebellion, for it seemed Diabolus would never be able to silence Conscience. But Diabolus could see that one moment Con-science would tell the people they had to do one thing, and then quickly contradict himself. This left everyone confused about what they had to do – or not do – to be good citizens.

"There is no longer any need for you to catch him," Diabolus told his angels. "His preaching will be to our benefit. With a little encouragement from you, Conscience will say that the King's Laws are not important. Go and see to it." He clapped his hands. "Hurry!"

The shadow angels poured from the strong tower where Diabolus now sat on the Lord God's throne, keen to do their master's bidding. I don't know how the shadow angels managed it, but it wasn't long before Conscience got fed up with deciding what was right and what was wrong, and declared it was just too much trouble to keep trying to please the King.

"Since the King is not here to see you," he announced, "you might as well do whatever you want."

"What happens when the King comes back?" a man asked. Clearly not everyone one was being taken in.

Conscience shrugged. "You can always behave more honestly and devotedly when he does." He smiled in a sly sort of way. "Maybe I should say, *if* he comes back."

Although this seemed to satisfy everyone for a short time, by evening we saw small groups of people crying, saying they had neglected their King. By early the next morning Conscience seemed to have thought things through. Maybe he'd spent the night remembering how everything had been so good and peaceful when the Creator God had been here. So Conscience stood up again in the market square, just as the sun was coming up over the hills.

"People of Mansoul," he called, "I can see now that we have done wrong in not serving the mighty King of Heaven."

Talora reckoned Conscience was wasting his time. Most of the people were still in bed, and she said he'd have done better to wait until everyone was up. But Conscience probably knew he was early, which is why he shouted even louder than usual.

Louder? This time his voice made the windows rattle right through the town, bringing people running out of their houses in panic.

The commotion must have woken Diabolus, for he hurried from the strong tower, joining what was already a large crowd of people in the market square.

"Conscience has gone mad," Diabolus explained to the people around him, when he had their attention. "He tells you to do something one moment, and tells you the opposite the next. What use is a madman like him in our town?"

That made some of the people laugh, and others quickly joined in. Indeed, it was obvious that most of the people now considered Conscience not only mad, but a real nuisance. No one seemed to notice that Diabolus had referred to Mansoul as *our* town.

A thin man we'd not seen before pushed his way through the crowd to Diabolus. "My name is Choosing," he announced breathlessly.

Choosing looked for something to stand on, but could find nothing suitable. He raised an arm and whistled to get seen, and in time the people became quiet.

"I was a friend of Conscience, before Diabolus came into the town," he said, in a thin voice that went well with his figure. "A long time ago, with help from Conscience, I chose to serve the Lord God faithfully and honestly. But now Conscience is nothing more than an object of fun all through Mansoul." He paused for a moment as though deep in thought.

"I hope Choosing has come to help," Talora said in dismay. "Oh, Zephan, I really hope Choosing is on the Lord God's side."

"I'm not so sure," I said. "I think he wants power. Let's see."

Diabolus put an arm round Choosing's bony shoulder in a friendly way. "Come to my tower in a few minutes, my friend," he said. "We can talk there."

As soon as Diabolus was back in his tower, smirking all over his face, Choosing knocked impatiently on the door. A shadow angel opened it and ushered Choosing into the throne room. Talora and I managed to squeeze in just as the door was slammed shut.

Perhaps I should explain in a little more detail why we were able to enter the room without being seen. As I'm sure you've remembered, this was a vision of the past, so we weren't really there – in a way – if you see what I mean. When you're watching a film or reading an exciting book, I imagine there are times when you get a bit worked up and want to warn one of your favourite characters about some danger. But of course you can't change what's going to happen, because the film has already been made or the book written. That's exactly how it was with us. And yet there was one difference. We could walk down the narrow streets, open and close doors, push our way through the crowds and generally feel we were really there. It's just that we couldn't speak to anyone, or change things.

"I come to promise allegiance to you, my lord and master," Choosing said to Diabolus, while we hovered high up in the room.

Of course we waited anxiously to hear the answer, even though it seemed unlikely that Diabolus was about to turn down the offer.

"You have chosen well," Diabolus said to Choosing, with a smile. "Come forward to my throne, Choosing, and I will appoint you Captain of my Castle, Governor of the Town Walls, and Keeper of the Gates of Mansoul. I will tell the people they must come to you when a decision is needed. Is that acceptable?"

Choosing said is was very acceptable, and I have to say he

looked ever so pleased with himself. However, far from solving all his problems by this clever move, as well as putting Understanding in prison, Diabolus found that the Keeper of the Law, Conscience, was still making a nuisance of himself. Even as Choosing was leaving the throne room, a shadow angel hurried in to say that Conscience had found copies of the Law of the Lord God and pinned them up in the market square. Everyone was reading them. Conscience must be punished severely!

Choosing hurried there and clapped his small hands. People turned away from reading the Law to hear what he had to say. However, being a thin man he was almost invisible to the crowd.

"Great and noble people of Mansoul," Choosing called in his feeble voice, standing on a large pile of logs and puffing out his arms and shoulders to look wider than he was, "listen to me. I am now Captain of the Castle of your new king Diabolus, Governor of the Town Walls, and Keeper of the Gates of Mansoul. You will do well to pay attention to my words."

Choosing's voice sounded stronger as he mentioned his new titles, and he seemed to have gained a little weight. Even so, I noticed that although the people looked up, most of them seemed unimpressed.

"We don't even know who you are," several men called out. You could hardly blame them. I don't think Choosing had been noticed much until now.

"For those of you who do not know me," he called back, "my name is Choosing. I am the new Captain of the Castle, Governor of the Town Walls, and ..."

"Get on with it and tell us what you want," a young woman interrupted.

Choosing turned red. "News has come to our new king that

copies of the Law have been discovered here in the market square. They must be destroyed immediately."

This didn't seem to present a problem. It was obvious that the people weren't too keen on what they'd been reading, and a small group immediately tore up the pages and threw the pieces over the walls. Scraps of paper fluttered to the ground far below, where the decomposing bodies of Captain Resistance and Innocence lay. Nobody wanted to go near them to bury them, probably because they felt guilty for allowing disaster to strike.

A shout from behind made Choosing turn round quickly as a shadow angel came pushing his way through the crowd. "Stop! I have here more pages of the Law. I have just discovered them … outside … the *castle of Diabolus!*"

The thin man who now claimed to be the Captain of the Castle, Governor of the Town Walls, and Keeper of the Gates of Mansoul snatched the pages and pushed them behind his back before anyone could get a good look. Quickly he left the market square and hurried to the castle. Once again Talora and I managed to squeeze in before the door was slammed shut.

"I thought all the Laws had been destroyed," Choosing complained to Diabolus. "It's difficult enough for me to choose on behalf of the people at the best of times, but if some of the Laws still remain …"

"I have good reason to believe that Conscience has several sets," Diabolus interrupted sharply. "He has hidden them in all sorts of places and will not tell me where. And there is another thing," he added.

Choosing waited. "Yes?"

"I am worried that Understanding's house still has some light reaching it. If the King tries to win back the town, I do not want trouble from people like Understanding. Get out now, go into the streets and hire a trumpeter to walk before you. Tell the people how great I am." Diabolus smiled one of his special smiles. "Tell the people I love them, and have no wish that harm should come to them." His voice and expression changed to one of cruelty. "But if they want me to protect them, they must *obey* me!"

CHAPTER 9

No-Truth

For several days we wandered through the narrow streets, watching Choosing and the trumpeter parade through Mansoul. The smell of the wild flowers that grew on the castle green no longer seemed so sweet. Brambles had started to spread their way through the alleyways and up the town walls. Worst of all, we were shocked to hear the people beg Choosing to tell them more about their new king, Diabolus.

One day, Choosing stopped at the Eye Gate and looked into the distance. For a moment he seemed concerned. "Wait. Can anyone see something suspicious on the horizon?"

No one could. Choosing hurried to the Ear Gate and listened through the trumpet, but heard nothing. I signalled to Talora and we flew high into the air. When you get up high you can see so much further. Anyone who has been in an aeroplane or looked down from a mountain will know what I mean. Just before you go into the clouds you can see all the fields and roads laid out like a map. Well, that's how high we went.

We could see nothing, but guessed Choosing was getting anxious that there might be a surprise visit from the Creator God. And well he might be anxious. The people were allowing Diabolus to destroy the Lord God's town, and they just couldn't see it. I wanted the King to arrive with his mighty army as soon as possible and put things right – as he surely would.

Choosing's next stop was the green outside the castle in the centre of the town. Here he discovered yet more pages from the King's Law, pasted on the walls of the surrounding houses. Some of the people had already seen them and were calling to their friends to come and read.

"It says here that the Lord God still loves us," they told each other. "What ought we to do?"

Choosing took one look at the notices and ran to Diabolus. "Those pages will have to go," he protested.

"Who put them there?" Diabolus demanded. "I blame you for this, Choosing."

Choosing said nothing, but quickly returned to the green and ordered that the notices be torn down and destroyed. To his horror, he discovered that the name of the Lord God had appeared on flags flying above the five gates to the town. Again, these were quickly dealt with, as an eager group led by Choosing pulled them down, all the while cheering loudly.

One afternoon, news came that the shadow angels had caught Conscience, the Keeper of the Law, pasting pages of the Law outside the stronghold of Diabolus, and they had now shut him in the dark house with Understanding. Talora ran with me to the prison where planks of wood covered the windows from top to bottom.

Although Conscience was shouting, we could only hear him when we stood close to the thick walls. No one walking past took any notice. I kept wishing we could get inside, but even if we could, we wouldn't be able to set them free – because this had all happened long, long ago.

Later that day I hurried with Talora to hear Diabolus address the people in the throne room. We perched high on an inside ledge from where we could see and hear everything. The crowd fell silent as Diabolus stood up. I noticed he no longer tried to hide his face or his dark armour. It was strange, but the more the people of Mansoul saw of ugly Diabolus, the more they seemed to like him. Even the children running around the streets were unafraid when he walked past.

"You need a new law," Diabolus shouted.

"We need a new law," the people agreed.

"And I know just the person to give it to you," Diabolus told them.

"You know just the person to give it to us," the people chanted.

"Please be quiet!" Diabolus ordered.

I really don't know why he bothered to say please.

"His name is No-Truth," Diabolus continued, calming down a little. "I have been teaching him many things, and he has become a most faithful follower of mine."

The people at the back stood on tiptoe to see this new person.

"No-Truth," Diabolus called, "come forward and receive the chain of office as our Keeper of Wisdom."

No-Truth bowed his head dutifully as Diabolus slipped a heavy gold chain over his head, onto his shoulders.

Diabolus smiled. "Now, tell the people what the new law is to be."

No-Truth, a small man I'd not noticed until now, jumped up onto one arm of the large throne so he could be seen. Diabolus knocked him off irritably, and one of the shadow angels brought a box for No-Truth to stand on.

"O people of Mansoul," No-Truth called piercingly, as soon as he'd brushed himself down, "you have no need to be afraid of this new law. It will give you peace. Do you want peace?"

Everyone shouted that they wanted peace. I think the

people were in such a good mood that they would have accepted anything.

"Do you want happiness?"

Everyone nodded. Yes, they specially wanted happiness.

"Do you want to be pleased with life?"

They did.

"Then I give you the new law," No-Truth called back, proudly displaying his gold chain. "If a thing seems good to you, it is all right to do it."

"Is that the new *law*?" a young woman called in amazement from the crowd.

"Certainly," No-Truth shouted. "And I repeat it. If a thing seems good to you, it is all right to do it."

"And if anyone tries to stop us?" the young woman asked, sounding really interested.

"Tell that person they are wrong," No-Truth replied, with a glum expression. "Remember, you are never to blame for what you do."

Everyone declared that they most certainly never wanted to be blamed for what they did, and Talora said she couldn't believe what she was hearing.

"Can the people be taken in so easily?" she whispered.

I told her that nothing in Mansoul surprised me now, but just made me sad. I must say the people seemed remarkably content with their new Keeper of Wisdom, and immediately voted for others to join No-Truth as his assistants. These assistants then reassured anyone who hesitated that it was true – they were free to live as they chose, without interference from any foolish people who still wanted to follow the Laws of the Creator.

Diabolus rubbed his hands in delight. I stayed with Talora, perched on the ledge as everyone left.

"I believe I am safe now," Diabolus told his shadow angels, when the people had gone back to their homes. "*Everyone* has accepted me, and as far as I can see the Law Books have been destroyed. Is that not so?"

The shadow angels said that the people did indeed accept him, and most certainly the Law Books ceased to exist. In fact, each copy had been not only destroyed, but completely forgotten.

Diabolus nodded in pleasure. "Does anyone in Mansoul still remember the days when they served the Lord G ..., the Creator?"

I held Talora firmly as the shadow angels below us rushed forward and knelt on the ground. Even though this was just a vision, Diabolus seemed so repulsive that I wanted to get Talora out of the room. Not that Talora needed me to look after her, but the atmosphere was so evil that perhaps I wanted her protection as much as she wanted mine.

"Well," Diabolus repeated, "does anyone in Mansoul still remember serving the Creator?"

The shadow angels remained silent.

Diabolus stood up and raised his arms in triumph. "I think not."

Their silence left me wondering if the shadow angels knew something that they were afraid to mention.

CHAPTER 10

Pyramids and Sand

Just as we were getting used to being in Mansoul, the town walls disappeared, sinking quickly into the ground. Talora looked as puzzled as I felt. The blue sky became black, with bright stars shining though the night. Then, just as suddenly as it had begun, the scene changed to one we knew so well.

We were in Heaven, gathered around the Lord God's throne, singing praises – with millions of other angels.

The Creator God called us to his side. "I have told you that the vision of Mansoul is just a picture of the past for you both," he explained. "Do you think you have learnt enough from it?"

"Is it over?" Talora asked, frowning.

I was about to ask the same question. Surely there were lots of things we didn't know, lots of things to learn about people on Earth.

The King smiled. "Zephan and Talora, you will be going back to Mansoul soon. But first I am going to show you something exactly as it happened on Earth, many years ago."

Now, this is hard to explain. I don't know how it happened, but we saw huge pyramids and sand by the side a wide river of dark green water. This certainly wasn't Eltor – not with all that water. Come to think of it, there aren't any pyramids on Eltor either, although we do have plenty of sand – red and orange sand.

What we were seeing would have been wonderful, if it wasn't for so many families in slavery. We moved in close to watch a father select a lamb from the family flock, but it wasn't just any lamb. He kept saying it had to be perfect.

But when we heard the Lord God telling the father that the lamb must be killed, Talora looked at me and cried. The father had to paint some of the blood from the lamb above the doorway of the house, and down the sides of the doorway. This didn't go down too well with the family at first. The lamb that the father had chosen was loved by the family, and as you can imagine, no one wanted to kill it. It was too special, loved too much. But the Lord God said it was the only way to escape from slavery to freedom.

With tears in his eyes, the father sacrificed the lamb and wiped the blood around the doorframe. This may be a story you know well. However, if you could see how much it hurt the father to sacrifice the lamb to keep his family safe, you would get a very small idea of how much the Heavenly Father loved his Son – the Lamb of God.

Talora wiped her eyes, and I had to dab at mine as the picture came to an end and we were back at the side of the Lord God's throne.

"And now," the Lord God said, "I want you to see what happened next, after I rescued my people from slavery in Egypt. I had given them a sign of my love. When they sacrificed the lamb, the blood of that lamb kept them safe and gave them freedom from slavery. But that was not good enough for them. They quickly forgot."

So now we were shown another glimpse of the past, a vision of the Heavenly Father speaking to his Son about the human race.

We noticed the King's eyes glisten with sadness as he spoke.

"I love Mansoul. I made the people to be my own. Yes, they have been foolish, but I intend to rescue them."

The Son held onto his Father the King, and they seemed to be one. "I want the people to belong to us," the Son said quietly.

The King raised a finger. "But the people have turned away from me, and found other gods. False gods made of wood and stone. So now I am sending messengers. Let us see if the people will listen to them."

Throughout the whole of Heaven, not just around the throne, we could hear voices singing and rejoicing as the angels realised the King still loved his people. Even though we were witnessing something from the past, maybe three thousand years before your time, Talora and I joined in with the singing. The Creator God was sending holy men to call the people of Mansoul back to himself.

"Zephan, I want to be back in Mansoul," Talora whispered, taking hold of my hand. "I want to be there when the messengers arrive." Then she raised her voice. "O Lord God, there is still much I do not know. Please let me see Mansoul again. And let Zephan go with me."

CHAPTER 11

The Helmet of Hope

As the light of Heaven disappeared – and the sky became black, then deep blue – I realised Talora was getting her request granted. The walls of Mansoul rose again from the ground. Diabolus was still there. We saw him standing on the town walls above the Eye Gate.

Talora heard it first, the sound of angel voices praising the Lord God in Heaven. I thought it was the sound of Heaven still ringing in our ears, but it couldn't be, because Diabolus heard it too. He wrapped his cloak around his armour and stormed back into the town. The people of Mansoul seemed far too busy to listen to anything from outside, and they carried on as though there was nothing to hear but the sound of their own voices.

The first messenger arrived in the early morning, with something written on a large sheet of paper. He managed to slip through the Eye Gate as the sun rose, and nail it to the door of the tower where Diabolus was resting.

Let it be known to the people of Mansoul that the great King is coming to call his people back. Remember the days when you served and loved the King, and follow him again.

You can't nail a notice to someone's front door without attracting attention. The noise of the hammer hitting the four nails brought many people out to read it – until Diabolus woke up and had the paper torn down. He ordered his shadow angels to catch and punish the messenger, but the notice had already served its purpose. The people trembled at the mention of the Lord God's name. Throughout the town we could hear voices whispering about the words from the King, as people asked each other what it all meant.

Within the hour Diabolus called everyone together. "That notice was a mistake," he announced in a loud voice. "You need not worry. The messenger has been dealt with."

This brought a gasp from the crowd.

"Be warned," Diabolus continued, "the King is no longer concerned for your well-being. He thinks you have disobeyed him, which is why he is coming here to *punish* you."

"To *punish* us? Then who's going to protect us?" someone called out in panic.

"I shall watch over you," Diabolus promised. "You have wandered too far away from the King for him to be pleased with you now."

This brought a cry of alarm from the people, but Diabolus was quick to calm their fears. "People of Mansoul, you know you can trust *me* for the future."

The people walked away slowly, talking with each other about whom they could trust. Then almost at once they brightened up. The King was far away, they said. Some even started to laugh, saying, "What's the use of worrying about something that may never happen?"

As Talora walked with me through the town, we noticed everything looked more dirty and uncared for than ever. Not that the people seemed bothered. They said it was better to live for the present than to let the future get them down.

The next day Diabolus called another meeting of the people, this time in the market square. "Who wants armour?" he called.

"Is there going to be a fight?" several men in the crowd asked anxiously.

Diabolus laughed. "I hope it will not come to that, but we must be prepared for an invasion. Now, who wants armour?"

The shadow angels looked excited to see so many hands going up. No-Truth, the new Keeper of Wisdom, stood on his box beside Diabolus, but no one at the back could see him. One of the shadow angels brought a taller box, which suited No-Truth perfectly.

"Stay where you are," No-Truth called. "You will *all* be armed before the day is out."

But in spite of this promise, most of the people seemed unsure they would get their armour in time to survive an attack by the King. They pushed forward in a surge.

"Stay back! Stay back!" No-Truth called again from his box, reaching down to grab a helmet from one of the shadow angels. "First, you will all get one of these – *if you keep back!* It's important to protect your head if the King comes with his army. We call it the helmet of Hope, and Diabolus has one for each of you. Wear it, and no matter what sort of life you lead, you will be given hope that things will work out all right in the end."

"How can you be sure?" a woman asked from the back of the crowd. I don't think it was the woman who had called out a few days before. Quite a few people seemed prepared to doubt Diabolus now. Two more voices repeated the question. I looked to see who had called, but from the faces it could be anyone, for all the people looked worried.

Diabolus turned round. "Is the Magnificent Great-Hopes here?" he called.

No one answered.

"Great-Hopes," Diabolus shouted angrily. "Where are you?"

Slowly the crowd parted to let a man dressed in rags stagger through.

"Ah, Great-Hopes," Diabolus said, "show this woman how to wear the special helmet you have designed."

The dishevelled man took the helmet from No-Truth and held it up for everyone to see. "While you wear this trusty helmet you have no reason to be frightened about the future," he promised. "Look, I will show you."

Great-Hopes put the helmet on No-Truth's head. It fell over his eyes. Everyone laughed.

Diabolus held up his hands to silence the crowd. "Do not make fun of the armour," he shouted. "It is *designed* to fall over your eyes. Is that not so, Great-Hopes?"

The Magnificent Great-Hopes said it was so. "The further it falls," he told everyone, "the less you will be able to see."

Diabolus pushed Great-Hopes aside. "That is right, my magnificent friend. If you wear the helmet of Hope, it is important you do not see what is before you too clearly."

I wondered if Great-Hopes should be called False-Hopes, because that was all he seemed to be offering. But I suppose great hopes give people comfort for the future, even if they're false hopes, like those on offer here.

The crowd became silent as Diabolus called No-Truth forward and snatched the gold chain from round his shoulders, and replaced it with a heavy breastplate secured by thick leather straps. "I have made this for you myself. It is of the finest steel. This breastplate will protect and harden your hearts, so the King's words can never reach you. You must be sure to wear it if you are to do battle with the King."

Even though he'd parted with his gold chain, No-Truth

looked proud as he put on the armour. Everything seemed too large on the thin body, but No-Truth wasn't bothered.

"Do I get a sword?" he asked, turning round to let the people admire what he must be thinking was his fine figure.

"A sword?" Diabolus cried. "A *sword*? Why, I have here the *finest* sword. It is shaped like a tongue, and I have set the end of it on fire. It will speak by itself, and it will speak evil. Use it, and use it often, and the fire of your words will spread fast."

No-Truth tried to jump in the air so everyone could see his armour, but he stumbled and fell backwards off his box. Diabolus looked so enraged that no one dared laugh. As soon as he was back on his feet No-Truth hurried into the crowd, strutting in his new armour. Diabolus yelled to him to come back.

"There is no time to lose," Diabolus told No-Truth. "More messengers are already on their way from the King. Get back on your box and stand still. I want everyone to see how to wear my armour. Why, No-Truth, you do not have your shield yet."

Diabolus took a large shield from one of his shadow angels. I moved forward to read the name engraved on it. *The shield of Unbelief.*

"When you hear words that come from the King, catch them with this shield," Diabolus told everyone. "And when you have caught the words, throw them to the ground and scuff them out. I know there will be times when it is difficult, but you must do your best to destroy every message from the King."

No-Truth stepped down from the box, safely this time, and walked forward.

Talora nudged me. "Just look at him, Zephan," she whispered. "He thinks he's marvellous, swaggering up and down in that heavy armour. But I think he looks funny."

"The people don't think he's funny," I told her. "Most of

them look as though they can hardly wait to have armour of their own."

"Not everyone," Talora said, pointing to the back. "Some of the people over there look as if they'd rather go home and think about it."

"*Come back!*" Diabolus roared at No-Truth, who was again making his way through the crowd. "You *still* do not have everything you need." He waved a wide leather strap in the air.

"What is it?" No-Truth asked nervously, as he made his way back.

"A small but important shield," Diabolus said.

A few people started to snigger, but not for long. They realised Diabolus was serious.

"It is for the mouth," Diabolus explained irritably. "Wear it tightly. Then, even if you try, you will never be able to call out to the King."

"Maybe the time is coming when we'll *need* the King to help us," a young boy said.

"Do you really think the King wishes to help *you*?" Diabolus jeered. "The King may *pretend* he wants to help, but I have already told you he is coming to punish you. Now, who wants their share of this beautiful armour?"

It seemed everyone did. The people tried to grab every item the shadow angels held.

"Be quick," Diabolus called. "Your enemy the King may even now be watching the town, preparing to invade Mansoul."

This seemed an unwise comment to make, for the people pushed forward harder, pinning many of the shadow angels tightly against the wall.

CHAPTER 12

Four Captains

Once things settled down, the shadow angels were kept busy handing out armour for nearly an hour. "Pass these back to your friends," they ordered those at the front. "Let no one go without."

The people at the back, who had not seemed all that keen to have armour until now, allowed themselves to be dressed up. Perhaps they thought there was little point in being different.

I stood with Talora, watching in horror as the whole town became armed. Talora said she couldn't see how the Lord God would be able to penetrate Mansoul now.

"O lion-like people of Mansoul," Diabolus called to the crowd, "will you be brave enough to help me fight against the King when he comes?"

A cry went up, assuring Diabolus of support. At that moment Talora and I heard a warning shout from the watchtower at the Eye Gate.

"Be quick, some men approach!"

As the people ran to the town walls, I flew high above Mansoul with Talora. We could see four battalions of soldiers marching towards the town with the sun behind their backs. Soon they were within shouting distance of the walls. Diabolus locked himself in his stronghold, saying it would be best if he stayed there – until someone gave him a full report.

The captain who led the first battalion had a voice that sounded like thunder. The people looked at each other and wondered if it was Conscience, the original Keeper of the Law. But no, they said, everyone knew Conscience was still in prison with their old Mayor, Understanding.

I recognised the captain. I think all angels know the names of the Lord God's mighty warriors. This was Captain Boanerges, whose name meant Son of Thunder. He held a large, dark flag with three thunderbolts painted on it.

A captain called Conviction led the second battalion. His flag was a pale gold colour, showing a copy of the Book of the Law.

The third captain now came forward.

"It's Captain Judgment," Talora whispered. "Look at his flag. See the picture of fierce fire?"

"And that's Captain Justice," I said, as the fourth battalion came forward to the gate. A soldier carried the flag for Captain Justice. The flag showed an axe cutting at the roots of a dead tree.

Then I realised that the people of Mansoul weren't looking at the soldiers or their flags, but had their eyes fixed on the horizon. They told each other they thought they could see someone watching from the golden haze of the sun.

"It's the King, the King!" they called in alarm.

No-Truth had kept his box with him, so he could be sure of a good view over everyone's heads. He stood on it, on tiptoe, and used the gatekeeper's telescope. After looking for several minutes he put the telescope down and turned to the crowd, laughing. "It's nothing more than a mirage in the heat," he explained. "You surely don't think the King will bother to come to *this* town!"

"Then why are the King's soldiers here?" someone asked.

"They have no business with Mansoul," No-Truth replied from his box. "Now then, who will help me destroy these men, so we can live in peace?"

Most of the people shook their heads. There seemed to be far too many soldiers out there.

Captain Boanerges marched to the foot of the town walls. "I have a message from the Lord God, the Creator of the Universe," he called.

The people on the walls put their hands to their ears in horror. I nodded to Talora. "If they've got any sense they'll listen."

"But they'll refuse." Talora guessed, and spread her wings to move to the top of the Ear Gate.

The people started talking grimly among themselves. Choosing, the new Keeper of the Gates – and all the rest of his title – came forward. "Go away and leave us in peace," he called down to Captain Boanerges. His voice sounded weak again. He was also as thin now as when we first saw him.

As soon as Boanerges started speaking, Choosing ordered the people to come away from the walls and hurry with him to the stronghold of Diabolus. This sounded interesting. I joined them with Talora. In angry silence Diabolus heard the full account of the army.

"*Fools!*" he shouted. "*Fools!* Did I not order you to be on your guard? Why did you dare go to the walls of my town to look at the soldiers? I blame you for this, Choosing. You had no right to look at the soldiers. Did I not warn you that the King was coming to take all of you captive? Hurry, make sure the town gates are well fastened. It is important for everyone to wear their armour." He turned to a citizen whose helmet of Hope was high on his head and slammed it over the man's eyes.

"Wear it properly," he ordered. "Wear it low, or you may learn things it is better not to know."

"Maybe the King is coming to keep us safe," a girl protested.

"Safe?" Diabolus snapped. "Safe? If you try to follow the King's commands, you will lose all hope of safety. Trust me, and everything will work out all right."

"That's the sort of thing the Magnificent Great-Hopes would say," I whispered to Talora.

"Great-Hopes with his false hopes," she added.

If the situation wasn't so serious I'd have smiled. A sudden blast from a trumpet made me jump. Yes, even angels can jump at unexpected noises, but not for long. Everyone in the town clung together in panic, then quickly recovered and ran back to the walls to see the reason for the trumpet. Diabolus went with them, saying it was time to silence those soldiers for ever.

Talora flew with me above the town as the four captains lined up below the walls, the trumpeter still blowing his summons to the people to come and listen to an important announcement.

Captain Boanerges, the Son of Thunder, spoke first. "I have come from the King with an offer of peace," he called up. "But I have orders to take Mansoul by force if you reject his offer."

That might seem like a very short speech to make after such a long journey, but the words echoed and re-echoed around the walls so that everyone heard them many times. It wasn't long before the whole town seemed to be discussing the meaning of the captain's words.

As the echoes faded, Captain Conviction took his place. He pointed to the book of the King's Law on his flag. "You have disobeyed these Laws," he called up to the people.

"Maybe we have," Choosing replied in his feeble voice, "but what will happen to us if we let you in? That's what we all want to know."

Captain Conviction seemed to have no trouble hearing him. "If you want forgiveness, tell the King you have been wrong in neglecting him. Then call to him for mercy."

Choosing exchanged guilty glances with the people lining the walls, but kept quiet.

Captain Judgment came forward with his flag of fire. "The messages we bring are not our own," he announced. "They come directly from the King. Do not take our visit lightly. If he wishes to do it, the King can destroy you all today. His offer of peace will not continue for ever. Take it now, and be sure of safety."

As with the other messages, the words echoed around the town walls and narrow streets for some time. Before the echoes had fully died away I flew down, landing on top of the walls where Talora joined me. Instead of answering the captains, the people turned again to Diabolus to hear what he had to say.

Diabolus said nothing.

Captain Judgment hadn't finished, and his message seemed to make Diabolus more afraid. "People of Mansoul," Captain Judgment called up in a voice almost as loud as that of Captain Boanerges, "do you want the King to punish you, as he will punish Diabolus one day? Come now, accept his offer of peace and turn away from your new master."

Diabolus strode forward and started to climb onto the highest part of the town wall, but when he got there he had to sit down. He looked frightened, and I think he sat down to make sure the people didn't see his legs shaking. Still he said nothing.

Captain Justice, standing slightly behind Captain Judgment, pointed to his flag. Everyone could see the picture of the dead tree and the axe. To make his message easier to understand, the captain called for the soldier with the axe to come forward. He touched a large, leafless tree close to where he stood.

"Do you see this tree?" he called. "It has no fruit on it, for its branches are dead. The King says you are like this tree. You have produced no good fruit. Watch as I take my axe to the tree and cut it down, for it is useless. Be warned, the King will not be patient forever."

The axe fell with a crash on the base of the tree. I watched in fascination as the Ear Gate shook on its massive hinges. Diabolus looked down in alarm from the walls of Mansoul, probably afraid the gate would open and allow the King's soldiers to sweep into the town.

The people whispered to each other that the shaking had started as soon as the four captains had begun to deliver their messages.

Choosing clapped his hands and called for a good friend of his, a large man called Won't-Believe, who boasted he could hold the gates firmly shut. Won't-Believe hurried to the Ear Gate and threw his large weight against it. The shaking stopped, the echoes of the captains' speeches died away, and for a time the whole of Mansoul became silent.

Won't-Believe climbed slowly onto the town wall beside Diabolus and shouted to the King's soldiers to be on their way. "You have come with angry words that we cannot understand," he told them. "It does not seem to *us* that you have come from the Creator King. All you say is nonsense. We have no place for men such as you in *our* town."

Diabolus told his shadow angels that he was worried the people would open the gate in a moment of weakness. If anyone opened the gate only slightly, he explained, the soldiers would be able to force their way inside with more messages from the

King.

"And then all will be lost," he finished.

I stayed on the town walls with Talora, talking to her about the love of the Creator God who wanted to help the people of Mansoul. We intended to stay awake, but somehow we dropped off to sleep in the early hours of the morning.

A long blast from a trumpet woke us with a fright. I was learning quickly that I'm not too good with sudden trumpet blasts. Well, we don't get things like trumpets on Eltor, where the only sounds are the rustling of drelgo leaves in the summer, and the steady roar of strong freezing winds throughout the winter.

Shouting and the cries of battle filled the air of Mansoul. Angels can wake up really quickly when we have to, so we spread our wings and shot off to see what was happening.

CHAPTER 13

The Siege

The King's soldiers – the warrior angels – already had the town under siege, but the people must have been awake before us and were prepared for the attack. Two of Mansoul's enormous guns, mounted high on the town walls roared out, firing cannon balls amongst the King's soldiers, causing several injuries. But the King's soldiers seemed fearless as they charged at the Ear Gate.

The four captains had brought huge catapults mounted on wheels, as well as giant battering rams. With the catapults they hurled huge rocks at the walls. Then with the battering rams they attacked the Ear Gate.

The sound of the crashing rocks made me want to get out of the way, so I took Talora with me to see what was happening inside the town. Certainly the people defending the walls seemed determined to put up a strong fight, while further back Diabolus screamed at everyone to fight harder.

"Remember, the King will show no mercy if his soldiers break into the town!"

The siege continued all day, until rocks from the soldiers' enormous catapults smashed the two cannons defending the Ear Gate. Several of Diabolus' best friends in Mansoul were killed in the fighting, while many of the people ran home to their families, afraid that the King's soldiers would break through the gate.

"Let us surrender," Choosing called wearily from the walls, as another huge rock smashed into the gate, making the town walls shake.

I'm sure Choosing wouldn't have said this if Diabolus could hear him, but Diabolus had gone back to his castle by this time.

"Wait," a man called loudly. "Diabolus may be right. Perhaps the King won't receive us. Perhaps we've been fighting against him for too long."

A murmur of agreement spread from citizen to citizen, leaving Talora jumping up and down in frustration. *Open the gates! Open the gates!*" she shouted, but of course no one could hear her. Then she shrieked in fright as the sound of thunder roared through the maze of streets.

"There's nothing to be afraid of," I reassured her. "It's Conscience."

No one had heard a sound from Conscience or Understanding for weeks, but when Conscience began to speak from his prison, peals of thunder rolled through the town.

It took only a few minutes for Diabolus to come pounding through the streets from his castle to discover the reason for the disturbance. As he opened the prison door to make sure his two prisoners were safely inside, another trumpet blast from below the Ear Gate announced a new speech by the four captains.

"People of Mansoul, surrender *now* to the King," Captain Boanerges called. "There is still time. If you continue to turn away from the King, Captain Justice has come to make sure you take the penalty for your rejection."

Choosing managed to push his way to the front of the

crowd lining the walls. Actually, this wasn't very difficult to do, on account of his being so thin. Would he decide to obey Diabolus, or would he obey the King? After all, with a name like his, I imagine he could have done either.

"We will allow you in, on one condition," Choosing called down to the four captains, after some thought. "We have new laws here, and we are content with them. We have made many alterations to our town. We do not want the King to change anything."

Captain Boanerges listened patiently to this offer from Choosing. "Mansoul," he called back, "you disappoint me. I thought you were going to say you were sorry for your disobedience to the King."

"There's no need for us to be sorry," Choosing retorted angrily. "Go away. Tell the King we won't be any trouble to him, as long as he leaves us in peace. There's nothing much wrong here."

"Nothing wrong?" Captain Boanerges cried out. "The King is not interested in bargaining with you. You have heard his message. If you are to be forgiven, you must accept his offer of forgiveness."

I noticed a commotion in the crowd as the large man who was called Won't-Believe pushed his way through to join Choosing. He'd left the defence of the Ear Gate in the hands of others. Seeing him coming, everyone jumped aside to avoid being flattened. Won't-Believe quickly understood what was going on, and turned to the crowd.

"I have come just in time to save you," he said breathlessly. "Do you really trust the word of these stupid men? A message of forgiveness from the King? What makes you think the King is going to forgive you?"

"It's what the messengers have promised," a boy replied

from the front of the crowd.

"How do you know the messengers are telling the truth?" Won't-Believe asked. He was as large and heavy as No-Truth was small and thin. "Does it sound likely the King will forgive you for turning your backs on him?"

The boy was not going to keep quiet. "The captains down there are telling us the King has the power to forgive."

"The King has power all right," Won't-Believe shouted at the boy. "The power to *punish*. And you'd better not forget it, my lad. Don't come calling to me for help when the King has you in his power."

Won't-Believe's voice was so loud that the four captains heard him from below the town walls. They gathered their soldiers together and moved away from Mansoul. I could see disappointment on some people's faces in the town, for I felt many of them wanted to disobey Won't-Believe and open the Ear Gate.

Diabolus looked overjoyed when he heard what had happened, but I took Talora by the arm and pointed to a lively crowd. In all the excitement, the heavy prison doors had come open. Maybe the voices of the captains had broken the locks. Understanding and Conscience had slipped out, unseen by Diabolus, but not by the people who now crowded round the two men in the market square.

Understanding and Conscience began to call to everyone. Unfortunately, Won't-Believe realised what was happening, and ordered some of the strongest men of the town to march on the meeting.

"There they are," Won't-Believe shouted, but he drew back as Understanding pointed an accusing finger at him.

"If it was not for *you*," Understanding shouted, "the people of this town would have allowed the King's soldiers to enter our gates. You have lied and deceived everyone."

Won't-Believe looked angry, and he had a lot of bulk to look angry with. "People of Mansoul," he called, "destroy these two men. Silence them for ever!"

Conscience continued to point at Won't-Believe. "Do you really think this big man is the way to peace in our town?" he asked the crowd. "I tell you, you could have been safe this very moment, but now you have turned down the King's offer of peace. You listened to this stupid man."

It wasn't long before some of Won't-Believe's companions joined in the shouting. Talora pulled me back as a fight broke out. Within a few minutes it seemed the whole town was rioting. Although some supported Won't-Believe, most of the people seemed to have taken sides with Conscience and Understanding.

Diabolus sent a troop of shadow angels to arrest Conscience and Understanding, and after a brief struggle he had the two men back in prison on a charge of stirring up rebellion. This time Diabolus put them both in chains, making it impossible for either of them to escape if the door came open again.

Early the next morning I was sitting with Talora on the town wall above the Ear Gate, when a piercing trumpet blast from below the town wall startled me – but not too badly this time. We looked down to see that Captain Boanerges had returned for one last attempt at calling the people of Mansoul back to the King. It was very early in the day, and nearly everyone was still asleep. This time the people took ages to gather at the town walls, and when they did, some of them brought stones to throw down at the soldiers.

"You poor people," Boanerges called up in his loud voice, which echoed around Mansoul.

Before he could say anything more, the people on the walls

started to jeer and whistle, and throw their stones. "Poor?" they shouted. "We're not poor. We have everything we could ever want here in Mansoul."

CHAPTER 14

Talk of Grasshoppers

Captain Boanerges waited until the people quietened down. "You do not know you are poor, for you do not understand the riches the King is offering. You do not know that he is generous and forgiving."

"Diabolus never said anything about this," Choosing replied in his thin voice. "As Captain of the Castle, Governor of the Town Walls, and Keeper of the Gates of Mansoul it is my job to decide who to let in and who to keep out. And you are definitely *not* coming in – because you are telling lies!"

"Would you rather trust Diabolus, or trust the Creator King?" the captain asked. "Why do you think the King offers peace? Is he afraid of you? Of course not. He offers you peace because he *loves* you."

This set the people thinking, and it seemed that the whole town became silent.

Boanerges didn't wait long. "The King is so great," he continued, "that to him you are nothing more than grasshoppers on the path. If you do not move out of his way, he will crush you under his foot. Can you really turn away from him when he offers you peace and mercy?"

"How do we know there really *is* a King?" Choosing asked, making others nod their heads in agreement.

"Have you forgotten him so soon?" Boanerges called from the foot of the town walls. "Look up at the sky."

Everyone looked up, expecting to see some great sign, but the sky looked the usual pale pink and blue of early morning.

"So what?" an old man shouted.

"Think of the stars at night," Captain Boanerges continued. "Consider how far away they are. Look at the sun rising over the distant hills. Are you able to control it? Can you stop the moon giving you light? Are you able to count the stars in the heavens? Can you control the waves and waters? These are the works of the Creator King, in whose name we come to you today. He loves you. I plead with you to give yourselves over to him and trust him."

Choosing was so moved by this speech that he was about to order Won't-Believe and his men to unfasten the great beam that held the Ear Gate shut, when Diabolus appeared without warning.

"*Stop that at once!*" Diabolus bellowed. Then he smiled. "O my friends, you have every right to fear the King."

"That's why we're opening the gate," Choosing called back.

Diabolus continued to smile, but it seemed to be a very forced smile. "You are right to fear the King. He wants you to be his slaves."

"No," a group of young men and women replied, "he wants us to be free. He wants us to live with him."

"Are you sure?" Diabolus asked. "Then why does Captain Boanerges talk of grasshoppers in the King's path? If you are so interested in grasshoppers, I can be a grasshopper to you. I can keep you amused with all sorts of tunes, so you can pass your time in pleasure."

I noticed the people look up quickly in interest.

"However," Diabolus warned, anger in his eyes, "I see that

some of you are not wearing your armour. You must protect your hearts with my breastplate. Make good use of the helmet of Hope. Place it well down on your heads. Wear it always, and at the end of your days all will be well."

Everyone seemed eager to listen to this advice, and the people who had left off their armour ran home to put it on. Before long everyone was protected against the voice of the King's messenger at the Ear Gate. The few words that reached them they caught on their shields of Unbelief, throwing them to the ground and stamping them into the dust.

Choosing had now made up his mind – or maybe Diabolus had made it up for him. He leant over the walls and called to Captain Boanerges, "Tell the King we would rather die than allow him to change our way of life."

As soon as the captains received this message, they and the King's soldiers withdrew. I noticed some of the people looked unhappy because Choosing had rejected the King, but their new armour quickly made them forget. While they wore their Helmets of Hope they could always hope that everything would work out all right. They could see no reason to concern themselves with the Creator King. Indeed, they told each other, they were probably much better off without him.

I wanted to pull the helmets off their stubborn heads and throw their armour over the town walls. I know Talora would have helped me. I wanted to smash their foolish shields of Unbelief and force them to hear the King's message. But, of course, there was nothing we could do to help, because as I'm sure you know by now, this had all happened long ago. It's just that angels feel great disappointment whenever we see anyone rejecting the King, the Creator God.

CHAPTER 15

The King's Son

The vision changed. I was back in Heaven with Talora, glimpsing a time far in the past. We listened while the four captains gave the Lord God a report on what had happened at Mansoul.

"I made that town and the people who live there," the Lord God told the captains, when the last one finished speaking. "I offered them peace and love, yet they will not hear me. I cannot allow the people to remain unpunished. There is a price that has to be paid for the wrong they have done."

The King's Son came forward. "Father, the time has come. I will buy their forgiveness with my life."

The King put his arms round his Son. "It breaks my heart to let you go. The gates of Mansoul are shut fast, and Diabolus is in charge. But I have no choice. You must grow up in the town as a child, and be part of Mansoul. There is no other way for the price for sin to be paid, than by your death as a sacrifice."

The angels drew back in dread when they heard this.

"My angels, you must not fear for my Son," the King told them. "He knows the awfulness of what lies ahead. And beyond the blackness there is a time of light."

Watched by several millions angels, the Father embraced the Son. "Do I love you, my Son, or do I love my people even more?" he asked.

"I am the Lamb," the Son replied, "to take their guilt and stain when I die in the town of Mansoul. Then they can be free."

I nudged Talora. "The Lamb," I said. "That's what that picture of the slaves by the green river was all about, when we saw a perfect lamb sacrificed, and the blood spread over the doorway for protection. That's why the King's Son is called the Spotless Lamb of God."

Talora nodded. Don't misunderstand me, I wasn't saying anything new, for all angels know this – but it seemed worth saying out loud.

A gentle singing started, turning into a great and beautiful song of praise. The Son had agreed to leave the safety of Heaven, to be born in Mansoul. The Son was going there to fight and to win a great victory over evil.

To see it now, brought fresh tears to our eyes. Maybe we started to understand it properly for the first time. No one can earn forgiveness, but people can accept it as a gift. A free gift that no one deserves.

The vision moved on swiftly. We watched the King's Son grow up in Mansoul; watched him teach the people in the countryside and towns. Many listened and agreed to follow him, but Diabolus was always there, watching, waiting for the time when he could silence the Son of the Lord God.

It was over so quickly. I clung to Talora in horror, and Talora clung just a tightly to me. The King's Son suffering with the whip and crown of thorns, before being nailed through his hands and feet to the cruel Cross. Death, the darkness of the sky – and then the Son's victory over death. The joy of seeing him rising from the garden tomb, teaching his followers one last time, then returning to Heaven in triumph.

Suddenly the vision was over, and we found ourselves wide

awake in the shade of the large rock, back on the planet Eltor where we had started out.

"It was so real," Talora whispered, in tears. "So very real."

I held her hand tightly. "It *was* real."

"He suffered so much, Zephan. The Lamb of God, sacrificed to pay for the sins of the people. It's such a strange Universe." Talora dabbed at her eyes, but I could still see tears sparkling in the corners. "Here on Eltor there's only peace. On Earth I think there's nothing but war."

"War, disease, disaster," I agreed.

Talora nodded. "But the vision has helped me understand more about the Creator's love for his people. You told me you'd been to the real planet Earth. Is there *really* a town of Mansoul?"

The voice of the Lord God spoke again across the hot red and orange sand of Eltor. "*Why do you not ask* me, *Talora?*"

Talora smiled and shook her head. "I'm sorry, Lord God," she said. "I forgot you had given the vision for a special reason. Do we know enough to serve you on Earth?"

"*Know enough?*" the Lord God asked gently. "*You ask me if there really is a town of Mansoul, and then wonder if you know enough! What do you think, Zephan?*"

I swallowed hard. "I know, Lord God, that it wasn't just a dream – but please explain more."

The loving voice of the Lord God came across the hot sand of Eltor. "*Zephan, you only saw things as a picture. However, my people* are *Mansoul, and they are indeed like a town. Tell Talora what you saw when you visited Earth.*"

I looked straight at Talora. "I asked the angel who was guiding me where the people were. I wanted to see if they looked like angels."

"But without wings," Talora whispered.

I laughed, but not very loudly. "Yes, without wings. I saw people and castles. The angel told me each person is really like a small castle."

"What do you mean?" Talora asked.

I jumped up in excitement. "I understand now. Each person on Earth is like a miniature version of Mansoul. They can shut their doors and never let the Lord God inside."

"*You have spoken well,*" the Creator said. "*Do you want to help me enter those castles?*"

The planet Eltor became hushed as we thought back over the vision. Diabolus and his followers had been terrible. It would surely be dangerous to meet them face-to-face in real life.

"*There are two castles on Earth where you can help,*" the Lord God said. "*Castle Nadia and Castle Max. They are young castles, and there has been much prayer for them. Like the people of Mansoul, each castle has the freedom to choose.*"

"Choosing," Talora said. "Is *he* there?"

I think Talora meant it as a joke, but was this the right time for humour? The Lord God had a quick answer.

"*Talora, you are right. Choosing and his companions are there, living around the castles, whispering to the owners. Sometimes they make a great nuisance of themselves. I, too, knock on the doors of people's lives. I can gain entry only if I am invited in, but many doors are tightly sealed, and the owners put up much resistance to change. Soon you will understand more.*"

"When do we go to Earth?" Talora sounded astonishingly eager. I wasn't sure she fully understood what we'd just been told about the danger.

"*You start immediately,*" the Lord God replied. "*My Son will lead the attack, but you will not be able to enter any*" *castles. That is not for angels to do. But you can, if you wish, listen from outside to what is being said – and I am sure there will be times when this is exactly what you will do. Take no fear, I am far mightier than my enemy. I am the Creator God, the Lord God Almighty, maker of Heaven and Earth."*

We stood on the rock, two ordinary angels on the planet Eltor. The twin suns of Caspar had already dropped low in the crimson sky, ready for nightfall. We took one last look at the dark, fiery sky and closed our eyes.

The sound of voices made us open them quickly. Again the sky had become blue, but the ground felt different than it had in the vision of Mansoul. It was now soft to the touch, green grass and brown soil. I pulled at a handful of long grass. "This is real," I said to Talora, as the blades came away in my hand. "We really *are* on Earth."

We looked around in alarm. To have seen the Earth in a vision was one thing, but to be here now was almost too scary.

"Where are you, Lord God?" I called in panic, surprised I could no longer feel the love of the Creator as we could on Eltor. Surely we hadn't been deserted on this strange planet called Earth.

CHAPTER 16

Danger!

Close to us we could see two small castles, both flying white flags. Well, to be precise, the nearer one, which was in a dip, was flying a white flag. The other – a very smart castle on a high rock – had a white flag just peeping up on top, although it was still rolled up. These weren't massive castles, each one was just a small keep.

The keeps were all shapes and sizes, although most of them were more like watch towers. Each castle had a single door, and the windows were often high up for safety. Mansoul had been a town where many people lived. We now knew that just one person lived in each of these castles, although clearly not everyone was home. We could see people of all ages coming and going, chatting with each other and laughing. Most of them seemed happy enough with life. Some had even left their doors wide open when they went out.

We walked towards the smart castle, the one on the rock. It looked so much better than the one in the dip, even though the one in the dip was flying a white flag on a high pole. The walls of that one had been poorly built, and it wasn't even in a position where it could be properly defended. What sort of person lives in a castle in a hollow, instead of one on a mound for protection? I was amazed the flag hadn't blown down in the first winter gale, taking the castle with it. I decided the place might be tougher than it looked, and was probably Castle Nadia.

The castle in front of us seemed to be superbly built, and someone had chosen a great place for it. Not only was it on high ground, it had been built on a rocky outcrop. The large blocks of stone in the walls fitted tightly. With such a strong doorway, this must be Castle Max. I felt sorry for Castle Nadia, which would need a lot of defending if the enemy came.

I pulled Talora to the ground. "Let's make sure we can't be seen," I whispered.

"We were invisible in Mansoul," she reminded me.

I had a feeling things were different now. "Don't forget Mansoul was just a vision. We could be in serious danger here."

"I thought angels are invisible to people," Talora countered.

I glanced around warily. "I'm not taking any chances. Imagine what would happen if people were able to see our wings."

Angels are pretty sharp when it comes to knowing things. We have an in-built knowledge. Of course, we don't know everything, which is why I was wondering if anyone could see us now.

"You're right," Talora agreed, now sounding a little anxious. "Let's get off the path."

Slowly, so as not to attract attention, we made our way through the long grass to some bushes where we could shelter – and keep an eye on the strong building I thought was Castle Max.

After a few minutes I felt braver, and decided I'd been worrying about nothing. We were, after all, angels. It was time to spread our wings and get a view from high up. "Fly with me," I said. "It's best if we stick together."

Once in the sky we hovered and looked down. From up here we had a clear view over the whole countryside. Much of the area seemed pleasant, with fields and valleys where wild flowers grew. Massive outcrops of rocks and low hills broke through the ground, with small castles everywhere. It surprised me to see just how many of these castles stood in poor positions for defence.

Behind us was a long ridge, Shadow Hill, with a wood of thin and sickly trees moving across the top, like a dark, giant caterpillar. The Shadowed Wood. Don't ask me how I knew these names. As I've said, angels just know things. But you wouldn't need to be an angel to sense the Shadowed Wood was not a good place to visit.

In the other direction we could see the River. I must make it clear that this wasn't an ordinary river. It divided the land, where the Lord God lived, from the land of people. Beyond it, in the far distance, we could see the golden hills of Heaven.

Over to our right I noticed large areas of brambles, swampland, steep rocks, and unfenced holes in the ground, all looking treacherous. Amongst the trees of the Shadowed Wood I thought I saw some movement, but I was more interested in the castles than the wood.

Talora let out a sigh of admiration. "What amazing buildings these castles are."

I agreed. "I hadn't expected so many. And to think each castle is really part of a person."

"It's how the Lord God wants us to see people," Talora reminded me. "Each castle must be like the person who lives there. Old castles have old people in them. See that old man over there? His castle looks ready to fall down."

The Lord God had said we'd be able to understand life on Earth if we saw things this way. All sorts of people, living in all sorts of small castles. Old ones and fairly new ones – and brand new ones that seemed to have been built within the past few weeks or months. And each one . . .

Talora interrupted my thoughts. "Have you seen the white flags?"

I'd spotted them as soon as we arrived, but hadn't taken much notice. As we rose gently on a current of warm air I looked down at the smart castle, with its flag still rolled up on the pole. The white flag on the poor castle in the dip flew high, although the light breeze made the pole bend this way and that. Was the flag a sign of surrender? That was when I realised that all the flags had the same picture on them.

"A dove," I said slowly. "What do you think it means?"

"Definitely a dove," Talora agreed, flapping her wings gently to maintain height. "It must be a picture of the Holy Spirit, to show that he lives there. That one in the dip is one of *his* castles!"

I felt sure Talora was right, and it made me excited to know there were castles belonging to the King so close to us. In some places we noticed groups of castles flying these flags. In other places the white flags were in ones and twos, but many, many castles were without flags.

"Well," Talora said, pointing to the castle on the rock, "Castle Nadia certainly looks strong."

I shook my head. "I think that's Castle Nadia down there in the dip."

Talora flew closer to the castle and shook her head. "It says Castle Nadia over the doorway. And see, the door is open."

I frowned. "Is it all right to go in?"

"No, Zephan, we've been told we cannot enter the castles."

"Then where's Castle Max? Maybe it's one of the other strong buildings over there on high ground. The Lord God wouldn't have sent us to the feeble one in the hollow."

Talora smiled. "Perhaps that's exactly what he would do."

Yes, I thought, Talora was probably right.

Talora pointed as she swooped down. "The door's closed, but if you look carefully you can see it says Castle Max on the stonework above it. The place doesn't look strong enough to be a castle."

I felt shocked by its frail looks. A white flag high on a bendy pole, no defences worth speaking of – this was the sort of situation where all you can do is trust the Creator God.

Castle Max and Castle Nadia were newer than many of the castles around. A rumbling sound from behind made us turn quickly as something large came out from the Shadowed Wood, raising a cloud of dust.

Talora grabbed hold of my arm. Angels can do that when we're flying, as long as we're facing each other and make sure our wings don't clash. "What do you think it means?" she asked.

"Riders on horseback," I said, hearing my own voice rise with unease.

"Are we in danger?"

I pointed to some dense bushes. "I've a bad feeling about this. Let's drop down there and keep out of sight – until we know who those riders are."

Once we were in the shelter of the large green shrubbery I raised my head, but not very much.

Talora cautiously raised her head with mine. "I'm glad we hid," she said, her voice shaking. "I can see soldiers, but they're not the warrior angels of the Lord God."

I frowned. "So why isn't everyone rushing back to their castles?"

Talora shivered. "I think it must be because they can't see

them. So why can we?"

That was when I understood. "Because *we're* angels and *they're* angels, Talora – *shadow angels* – and they'll see *us* if we're not careful. So let's keep quiet."

"I expect Diabolus has sent them to look for us," Talora said.

I didn't like the sound of that. "Don't say such things."

Talora gave me a comforting squeeze on the arm, but my main concern was for Castle Max. The building looked different from ground level, as things do, but no stronger. I could see Max on top of his castle, staring towards Shadow Hill. He must have realised something was amiss, but all he did was tighten the cord holding the flag high on the pole.

Talora pointed up to Castle Nadia, the one I now knew was the smart one on the raised rocks. "Look, Nadia's opening her door! Doesn't she feel any danger?"

I was looking at the top of Castle Nadia. The flag we'd seen from the air, rolled tightly around the pole, had now disappeared from sight. The shadow angels stopped on the path by our hiding place, close enough for us to hear their horses panting for breath. How had the King's enemies found us so quickly? Were spies of Diabolus here, passing on every bit of information?

"They'll see us if they come any closer. I know they will," Talora whispered.

"They've already seen us. See, they're leading their horses this way."

"God will protect us," Talora said confidently. "If he's placed us here to do his work, he will save us from harm." She looked up at the sky. "Lord God," she called loudly, making the shadow angels stop. "Lord God, in your name we ask you to come and protect us."

The riders drew back as the name of the Creator King filled them with panic. Even the horses started to pull violently at their reins, jostling into each other.

That was when we heard a distant trumpet.

CHAPTER 17

Five Captains

A cloud of dust on the horizon came closer and closer as more riders arrived. We felt a thrill of excitement when we saw them. The Lord God's warrior angels. Among a sea of bright armour and coloured banners sat the King's Son on a white horse, his armour of gold gleaming like the sun itself, the armour of his captains glittering like the stars in the heavens.

The shadow angels fled.

"Talora and Zephan, you must never be afraid to call for help." The King's Son leant down from his horse and spoke softly. "My enemy is powerful, which is why you can never beat him by yourselves. But against me he is powerless. Do not forget that."

The warrior angels of the King's Son seemed to number thousands. Horses and their riders filled the countryside, but clearly none of the people from the castles saw anything unusual. Then I heard a door slam shut.

The King's Son pointed at Castle Nadia. "You see, Nadia senses I am near. We may be sure her castle is well defended against me now."

"I don't understand," I said. "Nadia has a white flag on her castle. So surely ..."

"I don't understand either," Talora interrupted. "If you'd

been quicker you could have slipped through the door while it was still open."

The King's Son smiled. "I cannot trick my way inside these castles."

"But these people need you," Talora protested.

"Talora, I cannot go where I am not invited."

I glanced at Talora. Yes, we still had much to learn. The planet Eltor and the twin suns of Caspar seemed very far off now, almost a distant memory. I looked up at the King's Son on his white horse. Close to the King's Son five captains sat on their horses. These were not the captains who had challenged the town of Mansoul, but I recognised every one of them.

The first was Captain Trust, carrying a blood red banner with a picture of a Lamb. The second was Captain Good-Hope. His blue banner had three golden anchors pictured on it. The third captain was called Love. His banner showed a group of young people being held securely by the King's Son.

Captain Innocent was the fourth. We had to wait for his white banner to blow in the breeze before we could see the picture showing three golden doves. Captain Patience, the last captain on horseback, held a banner showing tears shed by the King's Son as he waited and cried for the people he loved to turn to him.

"Zephan," Talora kept her voice low, "why do so few castles fly the King's flag?"

"Because they don't know about the Lord God," I explained. "Maybe it will change soon. Look, the King's Son is going up to Castle Nadia. Let's see what happens."

Talora still seemed anxious. "Do you think the shadow angels will be back?" she asked, looking towards Shadow Hill.

I nodded. "I'm sure they will, but probably not yet." I watched closely as the King's soldiers formed a circle around

Castle Nadia.

"We should be doing something," Talora said, when the circle was complete. "The Lord God wanted us to help, not stand around watching."

"There's nothing for us to do. The King's Son is in charge."

"Maybe we'll be needed soon," Talora suggested. "Stay with me, Zephan, just in case."

I thought Talora was to be commended for her enthusiasm. Perhaps she was sounding braver than she felt. She certainly sounded bolder than I felt at that moment. The shadow angels were unlikely to be far away. It was time to join the King's Son at Castle Nadia. As I hurried there with Talora, a loud trumpet blast sounded from amongst the King's soldiers. This time I didn't jump at all.

Nadia appeared at one of her high windows. From up there the army of the King's Son would surely seem an awesome sight, but Nadia only frowned, obviously unable to observe anything unusual.

We could see what Nadia couldn't. From the castle as far as the horizon, thousands upon thousands of the Lord God's warrior angels stood ready for action.

Just this side of the River I could see two hills. The King's Son turned to us as we approached him. "The hill on the right is called Mount Freedom," he explained. "The other is Mount Justice."

Slowly the soldiers hauled four enormous wooden catapults onto these two hills. Then they took a golden battering ram towards the castle. These war machines were exactly what we'd seen in the vision of Mansoul – where they'd done serious damage to the town defences.

I turned to the King's Son in surprise. "It looks as though you're going to smash your way into Castle Nadia," I said. "You told us you can only go where you're invited."

"Wait and see, Zephan," the King's Son replied quietly.

From inside the castle we heard a shout of panic. Nadia must now be able to sense something of what we could see, and it sounded as though she didn't like it. She rushed to the top of her castle, struggling to pull the white flag higher up the pole. The flag opened, went up a short way, then stuck. This was the first time I'd seen Nadia's flag unfurled. Whatever picture it had on it, it didn't look much like a dove. It was more like some strange bird Nadia had drawn herself – but not very well. Then Nadia shouted down to Castle Max in the dip that she was about to be attacked. However, there was no longer any sign of Max.

"Do you think I am doing nothing to help Nadia?" the King's Son asked us, when he saw our puzzled faces.

"I know you love your people," Talora said. "It's just that we don't know what's happening."

"Then hurry down to Castle Max, but return to me as soon as you understand how I need people to help me in my work. I shall be waiting for you on Mount Freedom."

Of course I wanted to stay and see what was going to happen at Castle Nadia, but orders are orders, and I've already told you that we chose obedience at creation. A gentle rain started to fall in the dip as we walked towards Castle Max, but it soon cleared. One thing I have to say in favour of the castle's position – the rain kept it remarkably clean.

Why were we walking? You may be wondering why we didn't swoop down on Max. Well, he probably wasn't used to seeing angels land without warning outside his door, and I wasn't convinced we'd be invisible.

Max was sitting on the grass in front of his castle, so it was just as well we'd been careful. Or was it? He didn't look up, so we probably were invisible. It may not be polite to listen to other people's conversations, but something felt good. Angels are quick to sense things – good things and bad things.

Five friends sat with Max, and they'd arranged themselves in a circle. I learnt later that this is how close friends often sit when they're talking with the King's Son. And we could feel the King's Son here listening – even though we couldn't see him.

In short, Max and his friends were asking the King's Son to come to Nadia to take her to be his own. And to come to their other friends. We could hear Max and his group naming them one by one. James and Sophie were just two of the names. For some reason these names stuck in my mind. Maybe we'd see them later. Now we understood the words of the King's Son. He did indeed need people like Max and his friends to help him in his work on Earth, by praying for their friends.

The words of Max and his friends really moved me, and through my tears I noticed Talora was also crying. I wouldn't want anyone to be surprised to know angels cry. We feel for you when things go wrong, and the same when things go well – although of course we can't love you as much as the King's Son loves you. He has a very special love for you that he doesn't even have for his angels.

Talora began pulling at my hand. "Come on, Zephan. Now we've seen Max we must go back quickly to the King's Son on Mount Freedom. Those were our instructions."

This was the first time we'd seen Max close up. I'm not too good at judging people's ages, because angels tend to see things as being thousands or even millions of years old. But Max was probably about the same age as Nadia.

The Lord God said we were here on Earth to help Max and Nadia. Well, Max didn't seem to need our help right now, but I looked forward to meeting him properly some time soon.

CHAPTER 18

Nadia

When we reached Mount Freedom and stood with the King's Son and his soldiers, we noticed Max was already back on the top of his castle. Nadia shouted to him that she thought the King's Son was getting ready to make a nuisance of himself – again. Even at this distance we could hear them both clearly. I didn't realise angels had such good hearing.

"Look at the soldiers' flags," Nadia called out. "And look at their glittering armour and the banners. What does the King's Son want with *me*?"

I'm not sure exactly what Max saw or heard, but it was enough to make him raise his hands in excitement. For a moment Nadia became hushed as the soldiers hoisted a huge white flag on Mount Freedom. Then she called even louder to Max for help.

Max called back that it was time for Nadia to surrender. This seemed to make her angry, and she pointed to her flagpole.

"See this flag?" she shouted. "One like this was good enough for the rest of my family – and this copy is good enough for me. I just wish everyone would go away!"

At the time I wasn't too sure what Nadia meant. Her flag was clearly some sort of fake, but she seemed to think it was all right to fly whenever it suited her, because it looked something like a genuine one.

I stood with Talora on Mount Freedom waiting to see what was going to happen, but the King's Son and his soldiers remained with us. Max and Nadia started calling to each other again. From the sound of Max's voice, I would say that the sight of the army didn't bother him at all. In fact, he sounded really welcoming. But darkness was falling and we weren't going to see much more until morning.

"What does your large white flag mean?" Talora asked the King's Son, as soon as night came.

The soldiers had lit a large fire on Mount Freedom, and we sat round it warming ourselves. At times the flames rose high, sending flickering shadows along the walls of Castle Nadia and Castle Max in the distance. Inside both castles all seemed quiet.

"My flag shows I am offering peace and forgiveness," the King's Son explained. "But my enemy has sent many false messages to Nadia, turning her against me."

"*Diabolus*?" Talora asked. "Is *he* living here?"

The King's Son shook his head. "No, he is not living here, but he has sent his messengers to many castles in these parts. You saw in the vision how he tricked his way into the town of Mansoul."

"Are you going to invade Castle Nadia?" Talora asked, trying to put on a brave smile.

I felt safe here on the hill by the firelight, especially as the King's Son was still wearing his golden armour.

"Talora, I have already told you, I cannot go where I am not invited."

I looked at the King's Son. "Then why the battering ram and catapults?" I didn't want to make a nuisance of myself, but I thought it was a reasonable question to ask.

The King's Son pointed to one of the huge catapult machines. "Even if I knock loudly, the only person who can open the door to me is Nadia, the owner. Be patient, Zephan, and tomorrow you will see why I have brought these weapons."

The fire crackled as long flames leapt up into the night sky. I thought the King's Son looked sad. "Nadia has seen my white flag here on Mount Freedom," he said after a long pause. "I want her to know that I have come to offer forgiveness, just as I gave it to Max."

I should have realised sooner – Max had already surrendered to the King's Son. No wonder he looked welcoming when he saw the Creator God's army. And Nadia? I'd suspected from the start something wasn't right about her flag. It was homemade, copied from one that belonged to someone in her family, and only raised when it suited her to look as though she'd surrendered to the King's Son. It was obvious when I thought about it. And there was me thinking angels knew everything without needing to be told!

"Tomorrow I shall leave this white flag flying on Mount Freedom, and raise another on Mount Justice." The King's Son sounded less gentle now. "A red flag."

I watched the flames dancing and playing in the middle of the fire that was getting larger and larger as the warrior angels threw more wood onto it. Yes, I could understand why the King's Son felt so sad for Nadia, but the thought of a red flag on nearby Mount Justice didn't sound at all comforting.

Before the sun shone over the landscape, before people in the nearby castles began to stir in the grey misty dawn, both Max and Nadia were up on top of their castles. They saw it before I did, the red flag hoisted on Mount Justice. As the sun rose in the fiery sky – a sky that Talora said reminded her of mornings on the planet Eltor – the flag on Mount Justice looked as red as the twin suns of Caspar.

"Zephan, Talora."

We heard the King's Son calling us, and hurried to find him. "You are to go to Castle Nadia," he told us, as he sat on his white horse in his golden armour. He reached down and put a strong arm around Talora. "Nadia does not understand the meaning of the flags I have raised on these hills. If she asks, tell her the flag on Mount Freedom means I am making an offer of forgiveness."

"And the red flag on Mount Justice?" Talora asked.

"The flag of punishment. The red flag shows Nadia what she deserves. The white flag of forgiveness shows her what I am offering. Forgiveness cannot be earned. It is free – if she will only accept it."

Talora nodded, and took me by the hand. Slowly we started to walk towards Castle Nadia, until the army of the King's Son seemed far behind. Nadia called down to us from the top of her castle. "You look like two very holy people. I hope you've not come to preach to me!"

I put my hand to my eyes to shield them from the bright sky as I looked up at the tower. "She can see us," I said quietly to Talora, "but she doesn't know we're angels. She thinks we're just visitors."

"Are you part of what's going on out there?" Nadia called down.

"The King's Son is making you an offer," I shouted. "You have a choice. You can accept ..."

"I can't hear you."

I tried to shout louder, but Nadia seemed strangely deaf.

"She's too high up," Talora told me. "I don't think she's ever going to hear us."

The face at the top of the wall disappeared. I looked at Talora and shook my head. And that was when someone wearing a loosely fitting cloak, concealing every feature, raced out through the castle door.

CHAPTER 19

The Magnificent Great-Hopes

I turned away. "We're never going to get Nadia to hear us. Let's go back to the King's Son." That was as far as I got. I struggled as the person from the castle grabbed hold of me. Then the hood of the cloak came away from her head and I saw Nadia's face. She looked furious.

The next moment she had us tied up securely. I can't say how she did it, because it all happened so quickly. That was when I realised that although angels are strong, we can't push people around.

"What are you doing here?" Nadia demanded.

I managed to pull myself upright, although Nadia held us tightly by the arms. Strangely, she didn't seem to notice our wings.

"We came to tell you about the flags," I said breathlessly, struggling to break free.

"If you have anything to tell, you can tell it to the Magnificent Great-Hopes. He's in charge here," Nadia snapped.

"Great-Hopes?" I asked in surprise.

Nadia spoke indignantly. "Have you never heard of the Magnificent Great-Hopes?"

"Yes, I've heard of him," I said. "We met him in Mansoul. He had the helmet of Hope. As far as I can remember he wasn't that magnificent."

"I remember him too," Talora added. "Magnificent? He's nothing compared to the Lord God, the King of the Universe."

Nadia became silent, but she still gripped us tightly. I noticed that the mention of the Lord God's name made her embarrassed, and for a moment I thought she looked unhappy.

Then, without another word, Nadia pulled us round to the back of her castle, our heels dragging along the soft ground. Now, if we'd been people, Nadia would never have been able to do this. I think angels must be a lot lighter, although I've never tried picking anyone up to check. Anyway, Nadia didn't seem to notice how easy it was to pull us along. Maybe she was too angry to think about it. Round the back of the castle we saw a line of small tumbledown buildings, old shacks or sheds really, packed tightly together.

"Is Great-Hopes in one of *those*?" I asked, and I suppose my voice sounded more than slightly mocking.

"*Silence!*" Nadia screamed. "Strangers are not allowed to speak without permission when they are near the dwelling of the Magnificent Great-Hopes."

I kept quiet.

"*Zephan and Talora.*" The voice of the King's Son floated across from Mount Freedom. "*I have already said you will meet bad inhabitants here, as you did in Mansoul. These inhabitants are sometimes people, but usually they are thoughts and wishes that whisper to the owners of the castles. There are good ones that come from me, and bad ones that are the companions of Diabolus. As you will discover, the bad ones have great influence on the people who live in these castles. I too heard many bad whispers when I lived here as a man, so I understand how powerful they can be. I will let you see them all as people, so you will know them for what they are.*"

Nadia sensed something unusual was happening, even though she couldn't hear what the King's Son was saying to us. She seemed uncomfortable, but all she did was hold us even more fiercely.

"Good morning, Captain Boasting. I've brought two visitors to see the Magnificent Great-Hopes," Nadia explained to a sentry who was guarding the door of the tumbledown shack.

The sentry flung the door open and Nadia pushed us inside. Talora tripped and fell, sprawling on the mucky floor. A man sitting on a rickety chair stared at us suspiciously.

"Well, well," he said slyly. "I am very pleased to welcome you to my palace."

Palace? If this was where the Magnificent Great-Hopes lived, it was far from being a palace. Just a dirty old shed with no windows. Maybe people can hope for anything if they can't see what's going on.

"I am the Magnificent Great-Hopes," the scruffy occupant announced pompously.

I remembered him in the vision of the town of Mansoul, but of course he'd not seen us there. And he certainly hadn't smartened himself up in the meantime. This was the creature who promised all would be well in the end; whose great hopes were false hopes.

Nadia struck out angrily at me as I helped Talora to her feet. "Quick, you two, bow down before the throne of the high and mighty Great-Hopes."

"Bow down, bow down," a hundred voices seemed to call from out of the darkness, although I could see no one.

"Talora," I said, "stay on your feet. We have no one to answer to but the Lord God of Heaven."

Nadia shouted. "You are insulting my great and magnificent leader."

I managed to pull myself free. "Great-Hopes has been deceiving you."

"Nonsense," Nadia cried, while Great-Hopes sat without moving.

I turned to Great-Hopes. "On whose authority do you speak?"

"On the authority of a higher king," Great-Hopes said after a bit of thought. "He sends me regular messages."

"And do you know his name?" I asked.

"I have great hopes that he is the ultimate authority on life and death." Great-Hopes stroked his chin thoughtfully and nodded to himself. "I am not sure exactly who he is, but he sends me many messages of hope."

"His name is Diabolus," I said, and Nadia gasped.

"*Clear the room*," Great-Hopes shouted. "I will not be insulted like this."

Nadia knocked me to the floor.

As I got to my feet, Talora turned to Nadia. "I'm not afraid of Great-Hopes," she said quietly. "The King's Son is far stronger than he is. We're not afraid of Diabolus either. He joined the losing side against our King a long time ago."

Nadia stared open-mouthed, so Talora continued.

"You must listen to the King's Son, Nadia. He has bought you – with his life."

I could see that Talora had Nadia's attention.

"He loves you," she added.

The Magnificent Great-Hopes stood up from his throne – the old chair – his clothes hanging on him like rags. "The King's Son?" he snorted. "He will never force his way inside my castle. This is *my* stronghold. I have warned Nadia that the enemy is coming, and she does not wish my castle to be invaded."

"It's not *your* castle," I said. "It's the Lord God's castle."

"*Never*," Great-Hopes thundered. "You can tell your … your *King* … that I will have no dealings with him. Make no mistake, everything will work out all right for Nadia in the end. It does for everyone."

"You're deceiving her," I said, brushing myself down. The floor was filthy. "The King's Son is getting ready to attack. Soon Nadia will learn the truth."

Great-Hopes laughed. "*Truth*? To this castle the truth is that I bring great hope, and Nadia will learn nothing different. Who are you, to be doing work for your King?"

"We are servants of the Lord God," Talora said, standing tall and proud. "We shall obey him always."

The mention again of the Lord God sent Great-Hopes into a deeper rage. He pulled us out of the room and dragged us to the foot of the castle walls.

"You're going to the dungeon," he roared. "And you'll never speak to Nadia again."

The dungeon looked like a deep well. I could see several other holes that had been dug in the ground, two of them going sideways under the castle walls, bringing the risk of collapse. Castle Nadia was in danger, and Nadia either didn't know or didn't care.

A heavy metal plate covered the top of the dungeon. As Great-Hopes struggled to slide it sideways, Nadia bent down to help him. When the hole was open, Great-Hopes untied us and threw us both in. As we fell we weren't able to open our wings in time to stop ourselves landing with a painful crash far below. I looked up to see Nadia and Great-Hopes sliding the cover back into place. For a moment everything seemed completely black, but it wasn't long before I noticed a small amount of light leaking around the edges of the cover.

CHAPTER 20

Prisoners

I expect you know that dungeons are dark and they always smell damp. This one was not only dark and damp, it had a disgusting smell.

Great-Hopes – that is, Nadia's personal version of Great Hopes – had probably built it for her when she tried to discover the truth. It sounded as though there was always a Magnificent Great-Hopes to give encouragement to anyone who asked him about the future. Quite what people had to hope for he never got round to telling them, but constantly assured them that everything would be all right in the end. And people like Nadia probably listened gladly. It was an easy way to get through life.

I felt Talora jump with fright when we heard something move in the corner of our gloomy cell, and a feeble voice came from a heap of straw on the floor. "Are you prisoners too?" it asked.

"Who are you?" Talora demanded. "I thought we were alone."

"Alone?" the voice asked sadly. "You might as well be alone. Why, I can hardly speak, I have been silent for so long."

"Who *are* you?" I demanded.

"Who *was* I, would be a better question. I am not alone in this corner, you know. My friend here is even more silent than I am."

"Tell us your names," I said, going forward to hear the whispered voice.

"My name is C ... C ... Conscience."

"And your friend?" I asked.

"His name is Understanding," came the whisper. "We were both helping Nadia – a long time ago."

I remembered the vision of Mansoul, where these two had also been prisoners. Or maybe not these exact two, but two very much like them, with the same names – and with the same problem of getting thrown into prison. "I was wondering if I'd see you two here," I said. The King's Son had told us we'd discover whispered thoughts and see them as people. Perhaps they were part of Nadia's thoughts. I started wondering how many more of these "people" we were going to find.

"I ... I have not spoken for a long time," Conscience said quietly. "There was a day when this castle shook as I spoke. There was a time when I heard a voice saying to me, 'This is the right way. This is the way to go.'"

Even though it was almost completely dark, Conscience must have noticed Talora feeling her way along the wall of the dungeon. I suppose he'd been down here so long that his eyes had adjusted to the lack of light, and this made me wonder how he'd get on in the sunshine if we could find a way to rescue him. "What are you doing?" he asked.

"I'm looking for a door."

"Door? Young lady, the only way out is through the metal cover up there," Conscience said gloomily. "Great-Hopes has built this prison deep in the ground. It is not only dark, it has made me lose my voice. Even Understanding here in this pile of straw, even Understanding hasn't spoken for many months – although he's always awake. Without being able to use his eyes, he has no idea what is happening in the castle."

That was when I wondered why I was still standing on the dirty floor. I could fly up to the cover and push it away. "Fly up there with me," I said to Talora.

Well, it seemed a good idea at the time. But not only was there not enough room to spread our wings properly, the cover was much too heavy to move aside, even though we managed to cling onto an iron handle underneath it. I remembered how Great-Hopes had needed Nadia's help to slide it aside.

"You know Great-Hopes then," I said when I'd got my breath back, relieved to have found someone who might be able to help us do battle against the King's enemy. "I think he's been getting messages from Diabolus."

"Not only from Diabolus," Conscience said. "He sometimes gets messages from the Lord God, but he passes them on to someone called Choosing who decides what he wants Nadia to hear."

I remembered Choosing from Mansoul, a skinny man with a thin voice. Maybe he'd put on a bit of weight by now, but I had no wish to interrupt Conscience and Understanding. So for once I kept quiet.

Understanding got up slowly and painfully. I could hear straw falling away from his body as he brushed himself down. "I can tell that you are not from here," he said, in a voice that sounded weak from lack of use. "You have come from the King's Son. He is close to the castle – I know that to be so. He is at the door, is he not?"

"He's very close," I said. "We wanted to tell Nadia that the King's Son is coming with love, with an offer of forgiveness – but somehow we ended up down here with you."

Understanding moved closer. "There is a way out." His voice sounded stronger and clearer now. "By the time my friend and I discovered it, we were too weak to use it to escape. There is a small gap in the wall behind my head. I lie near it, so I can get some fresh air to keep away the terrible smell of decay. The passage behind it will be long and tight, but I believe it comes out somewhere under the castle walls."

This sounded exciting. I tried to push my way through the narrow hole in the prison wall and into the tight tunnel.

"Be quick," Understanding urged, as we heard a noise from the metal cover above.

I found I could just squeeze through, although my wings kept catching on the rough stone. The passage climbed up and up, becoming tighter and tighter, until the walls were so close I found it hard to breathe. Understanding could be wrong. Maybe this passage didn't come out anywhere.

I could feel Talora close behind me. "Keep going," she urged.

"There's no way on," I gasped. "I think I'm trapped. You'd better go back – if you can."

Talora wasn't giving up. "There!" She caught hold of my foot and gave it a hard push. "See that light ahead? Just keep going."

We squeezed our way on, past wet and slimy rocks, emerging from one of the holes I'd seen running under the walls of Castle Nadia. The bright light hurt my eyes, and a crowd of people rushing past nearly knocked us over as I stood up. Round here, flying was definitely safer than walking.

"Who are all these people?" Talora whispered, as she wiped the mud from our white clothes. Fortunately it came off easily.

Indeed, yes, where had everyone come from? They were about Nadia's age. I decided they must be her friends who lived inside some of the many castles around the countryside. I couldn't see Max.

"The Magnificent Great-Hopes is about to speak to the enemy," one of them told us excitedly, obviously not noticing our white clothes – or even our wings for that matter. "Are you coming to watch?"

Then, before either of us could answer, we found ourselves being whisked along by the crowd. Everyone seemed to be making for the door of Castle Nadia where the Magnificent Great-Hopes waited impatiently. He didn't notice us, which was just as well or he'd have thrown us back in the dungeon with Conscience and Understanding – probably in chains this time. Then, to much cheering from everyone, scruffy Great-Hopes made his way over the rocky ground and down to the valley to where the King's Son now stood, having left Mount Freedom.

"See brave Great-Hopes?" a girl shouted. "*He's* not afraid of the enemy out there."

Talora looked at me. "Not afraid? Look, he's shaking with fear before the Son of the Lord God. Come on, Zephan, if we fly down we'll be able to hear what they're both saying."

I had other ideas. "We can't let people see us flying. I can't understand it, but they haven't realised yet that we're angels."

Anyway, we found we could hear the conversation clearly from where we were, although a few of Nadia's friends had to run closer.

"I know that you are the Son of the Most High God," Great-Hopes told the King's Son, "but Nadia wishes to have no contact with you. I have treated her well with many promises, and she has no fear for her future. I beg you, go away and allow me to keep this castle for myself."

"Go back and tell Nadia I love her," the King's Son said. "Tell her I want to forgive her for everything she's ever done wrong, and then live with her and care for her, to fill her with my love."

One of Nadia's friends tugged my arm. "See? The man on the horse will be telling Great-Hopes that this castle is doing just fine, so he's promising to leave Nadia alone."

Well, she certainly couldn't hear as well as us, if that's what she thought was happening. This made me even more certain that angels have fantastic hearing. Or maybe we can hear things in some special way. I must ask sometime.

Great-Hopes finished his conversation and turned away, looking furious. He crawled back up the hill and spoke to Nadia and her friends in front of the castle. "People," the shabby man shouted to the crowd, "the King's soldiers out there have no love for anyone. Their leader says he is going to attack, and he will destroy anyone who puts up a fight. Be quick, defend Castle Nadia!"

"You're wrong. I heard him tell you that he's coming in love," a girl said breathlessly, hurrying back up the hill from where she'd been listening.

Great-Hopes shook his head. "You shouldn't eavesdrop on private conversations," he snapped. Then he seemed to think about it. "Well, yes, that may be what he *said*, but it's not the point. What he really *meant* was that he's coming to attack and destroy."

"Why should anyone attack Nadia?" one of her friends asked from the front of the crowd. "She's done nothing wrong."

"Let's send another representative to talk to the King's Son," an older boy suggested.

Most of Nadia's friends seemed to like this idea.

"I could go," a voice said.

Everyone looked to see who had spoken.

"I am Good-Deeds." A young man pushed his way to the front. "I have been ever so busy lately, helping Nadia to be a nicer person."

I have to say I thought young Good-Deeds sounded full of himself, but a murmur of approval swept through the crowd, and some of Nadia's friends started to clap.

"Good-Deeds will go for me," Nadia shouted.

Before long all Nadia's friends had taken up the cry, cheering wildly in support of Good-Deeds. I guessed he must be one of the best-known people in the whole country.

"Please allow me to pass," Good-Deeds said politely. "Nadia deserves my help."

I mentioned a moment ago that Good-Deeds sounded full of himself, but now his voice was changing to one that seemed ever so humble, although somehow it didn't ring true. I guessed he was really a proud young man.

"Make way for Good-Deeds," Nadia's friends shouted. "Make way for Good-Deeds."

We watched Good-Deeds run down the hill, a confident look on his grinning face. He obviously expected a good reception.

Once again we listened carefully.

"I have already told Great-Hopes that Nadia must surrender to me completely," the King's Son told Good-Deeds. "*You have come here to win my friendship by telling me of Nadia's good behaviour, but I have come to offer her forgiveness as a gift. Nadia can accept it or she can refuse it, but she cannot use you to buy it. Return to the castle, Good-Deeds, and tell Nadia that you count for absolutely nothing in my sight. And tell her that I come with love.*"

A sad looking Good-Deeds crept back up the hill to break the news to Nadia and her friends. He looked around, probably expecting to see Great-Hopes, but the shabby creature had returned to his equally shabby shed behind the castle.

Good-Deeds then called for one of his young friends,

named Unchanging. Everyone thought Unchanging would be a great choice. He would defend Nadia because he'd never once altered his mind about anything.

"Nadia must refuse to surrender," he shouted, and Nadia's friends immediately elected him leader.

Then, to our surprise, instead of going to the King's Son, Unchanging marched round to the back of the castle, keeping his legs stiff and straight like an old-fashioned mechanical toy.

"I must speak with the Magnificent Great-Hopes," he told Captain Boasting, who was still keeping guard outside the filthy hovel.

The captain blocked the door. "The Magnificent Great-Hopes will see no one," he barked.

Another soldier appeared. "What's going on," he demanded.

"Stand back, Captain Secure," said Unchanging, who had obviously made up his mind to see Great-Hopes, and wasn't going to take no for an answer. "It is vital that you let me in."

A voice came from inside the hovel, and Captain Secure nodded. "The magnificent one says you may enter."

I held Talora's arm and we slipped inside with Unchanging. We were good at that now, and we stood motionless in the gloom in one of the corners. Great-Hopes sat upright on the rickety chair he used as his throne, looking decidedly anxious. But he smiled when he heard that Good-Deeds had spoken to the King's Son, and that Nadia had elected Unchanging as temporary leader. And he smiled even more when he knew Unchanging was about to make a visit to the King's Son.

"I have a clever plan," Great-Hopes said, trying to sound cheerful. "Listen carefully, Unchanging. I will tell you exactly what you must say."

CHAPTER 21

Unchanging

We followed Unchanging as he strutted from Great-Hopes' so-called palace, round to the front of the castle. "I am taking a message from Great-Hopes to the man on horseback," Unchanging told Nadia and her friends.

A thin man clapped his hands. I knew immediately who it was. Choosing's bony body looked exactly the same as when we'd seen him in Mansoul. We'd probably have the whole gang here soon.

"Keep back, keep back," Choosing croaked, his voice as weak as ever. "Allow Unchanging to get through."

I shook my head and turned to Talora. "What's the use of sending Unchanging? He can't even bend his knees enough to get over the rough ground on the hill."

"He's fallen over," Talora said, laughing. "But look, the King's Son is coming up to talk with him."

I wanted to fly down to hear what they were saying, but Talora held me back. "No, Zephan, you were right just now. We cannot risk being recognised. Anyway, someone like Unchanging will speak so loudly everyone will hear. You wait and see."

Even in front of the King's Son, Unchanging refused to bow his head – or more likely he was unable to. "Great King," he said proudly, "rather than go to war with you, Nadia makes an offer of peace. You may take one half of her castle as your own, and the Magnificent Great-Hopes will rule the other half."

The King's Son shook his head. "The castle is mine. Search the ancient records, Unchanging, and you will discover that I bought these castles many years ago. I will not accept just half."

That's when I realised that although every castle had been bought and paid for by the King's Son, he couldn't take possession of them until the occupants surrendered completely to the King. It all made sense now.

Unchanging turned awkwardly to make sure Nadia, who was now on the flat castle roof, could hear him as she poked her head over the battlements. "I am authorised to make a further offer," he said. "You may possess the castle." He paused. "As long as the Magnificent Great-Hopes and his companions can keep just the smallest part." He smiled at Nadia's friends who cheered enthusiastically.

"The *whole* castle is mine," the King's Son insisted. "Go and tell that to Nadia."

Unchanging hadn't finished. "My master Great-Hopes is a very generous person. I am authorised to make a further offer. If you allow Great-Hopes and his companions to live quietly round the back of the castle, Great-Hopes will not claim to be king, and none of us will play even the smallest part in ruling this castle. We only want to live here in peace."

The King's Son shook his head firmly. As soon as Nadia's friends saw the rejection of the offer they began to shout and jeer angrily at the King's Son.

"Our leader, the Magnificent Great-Hopes, is willing to move away from the castle," Unchanging said hurriedly. "And we will go with him."

"That is good," the King's Son replied.

"Ah, yes," Unchanging added, "but you must allow us to

return from time to time to visit our old place for a day or two –
or a week, or even a month or two – whenever we are passing
this way."

"And why should you and Great-Hopes want to do that?"
the King's Son asked.

"Well," Unchanging explained, "there may be times when
our advice and friendship is needed."

"No," the King's Son said firmly, "I could never agree to
that. If Nadia invites me into her castle, I will come as the only
ruler. You and Great-Hopes and your other companions must
be banished for ever."

"You are a hard sovereign," Unchanging said. He turned to
Nadia who had come down from the roof and was now with her
friends outside the castle door. "This man has no feeling for
you," he called to them, and they started to jeer again.

"Will the King's Son leave now?" Talora asked. "I know I
would."

"Not if he loves this castle – and I'm sure he does."

The King's Son stayed talking to Unchanging. "How can you
come and go when your buildings have been destroyed?"

"*Destroyed?*" Unchanging looked shocked.

The King's Son sighed. "If I leave your old buildings at the
back of this castle, what is to stop you slipping back to live there
again?"

"Tell me," Unchanging said, still proud and unbent, "will
you require changes *inside* Castle Nadia?"

"If I am to come in, all trace of you and your companions
must be swept out."

Unchanging jumped back in alarm. "How could Nadia do
such a thing to us?" he demanded. "Why, no matter how hard
she tried, there might be some trace left in a dark corner."

The King's Son smiled. "Nadia is to leave the cleaning to

me. You are right, no matter how hard she tries she will not be able to clean her own castle, or her clothes. Not even your young friend Good-Deeds could do that for her – especially not Good-Deeds."

I noticed that Nadia looked badly shaken as she listened. Her friends told her it was unfair of the King's Son to talk about cleaning. Surely there was room for a bit of give and take, they said – a part of the old days left here and there.

Choosing shook his head sadly as Nadia's friends watched to see what he would do now. "This is a bad day for you," he told Nadia. "If the King's soldiers invade, you will be the most miserable of people. You and your friends must be strong and defend your castles – even if it costs you your lives."

With that, Nadia ran back indoors, noisily locking and bolting the door. I stayed to see what the King's Son would do next, while Nadia's friends swept Talora away as they ran around in panic trying to defend the castle door. There seemed to be no organised plan of resistance. A few minutes later Choosing and Unchanging clapped their hands and took charge.

Talora managed to break free, scrambling up next to me as the King's Son came close to the castle. He called out one last time to Nadia with his offer of peace and total forgiveness.

The door of Castle Nadia stayed shut.

CHAPTER 22

Mount Justice

Nadia's friends hung around outside her castle for the rest of the afternoon, while the King's Son returned to Mount Freedom with his soldiers. Nadia stayed inside, out of sight. I sat down with Talora in the shelter of some dense bushes, exhausted, intending to think things through. The dried leaves made a comfortable cushion, and we must have fallen asleep – rather like giskos in a cosy nest, I suppose.

We woke in the early evening to see five men in shining armour standing outside Castle Nadia holding flags. You may remember that we'd met them here earlier: Captain Trust, Captain Good-Hope, Captain Love, Captain Innocent and Captain Patience.

"It's looks as though the King's Son hasn't given up on Nadia," I told Talora.

"So why is she keeping her door shut?"

"Probably because she doesn't want to make any changes. We can blame Unchanging for that."

In the distance, watching from the shelter of some trees on Mount Justice, I noticed the four powerful captains who had visited Mansoul in the vision: Captain Boanerges, Captain Conviction, Captain Judgment and Captain Justice. I recalled Captain Justice, with his axe for cutting down dead trees. I pointed out the captains to Talora.

"I hope they're not coming here," she said anxiously. "Nadia is so stubborn."

As I looked around, I caught sight of Castle Max in the dip. I jumped onto a high rock in excitement, and without thinking used my wings to get to the top of it quickly. Fortunately, no one seemed to notice. "Look! Max has taken his flag down. Does it mean he's like Nadia, and only flies it when it suits him?"

"Nadia has a home-made flag," Talora reminded me. "Max has the real thing. Anyway, he's coming this way. And he's carrying his flag with him. That's why it's not flying on his castle."

Yes, that made sense. Max held his flag high above his head by two corners, and it streamed out behind him in the breeze as he ran towards Castle Nadia.

People came out of other castles that had been flying white flags, marching behind banners and carrying Swords. You'll notice that I'm using a capital S here. I'll be telling you more about these special weapons as we go on.

Some banners showed the white dove of the Holy Spirit, others had a crown, a Lamb, crosses – and a few had a fish, the coded message for the name of Jesus, the King's Son. Everyone marched up the hill to join the soldiers. Max stood boldly at the front, carrying his Sword.

The Swords weren't the ordinary weapons of war, but part of the armour supplied by the Lord God. Some people see the Swords as interesting but not very useful. Believe me, they are powerful weapons when used correctly.

At that moment I saw a great commotion between Nadia's friends and Max and his friend with the banners. Her friends who had been there all along, the ones without flags and banners, pushed their way angrily to the front. I thought there was going to be a fight, but Max and his friends stood back and kept calling out to the King's Son to be patient with Nadia. Then they called out loudly to Nadia to surrender. But Nadia's other friends shouted to them to be quiet, and told Nadia not to listen.

I have to admit I was shocked to watch the soldiers push the golden battering ram forward. But before using it they fired one of the enormous catapults, launching a huge rock at the castle door, scattering splinters of stone and wood. This hardly seemed like a loving approach.

Talora put her hands to her face. "We can't stand here," she said. "The soldiers are loading another rock, and I don't want to get hit in the eye by bits of wood."

I told her to stay where we were. We seemed safe enough, and I wanted to get a good view. "I don't understand it," I told Talora. "I thought the King's Son said he wouldn't force his way in."

"Look over there!" Talora had now uncovered her eyes. "Max and his friends with flags and banners are still calling out to the King's Son to help Nadia."

We watched as Max directed the soldiers working the catapults where to aim – no longer at the castle door, but at the hovel where scruffy Great-Hopes lived.

"And there's Nadia!" Talora pointed to a figure standing on the flat roof of the castle, leaning over the battlements. "I hope she won't keep the King's Son out for much longer."

The rock from the catapult fell just short of the Magnificent Great-Hopes' hovel. The rock shattered as it landed with a mighty crash that shook the ground, pelting the door with fragments of stone.

Great-Hopes came rushing out, ordering his two sentries, Captain Boasting and Captain Secure, to make his palace safe while he ran off to hide. Did I say palace? If you could have seen it you wouldn't have put a stray animal in there for the night, it was in such a state. As Great-Hopes rushed past, I put my foot out and sent him sprawling on the ground.

Several of the King's soldiers drew their bows. Captain Boasting, who was calling instructions up to Nadia on the best way to make the castle stronger, received an arrow in the chest. He dropped down dead. Another warrior angel drew his bow and hit Captain Secure. He fell to the ground outside the castle door, but the arrow had only entered his leg, and he rolled about in pain.

"We shall not be taken," he called to his companions, as he pulled himself to his feet. "You must all …" A second arrow hit him, this time in the heart, killing him instantly. He fell back, his eyes wide open in surprise.

"What am I to do? What am I to do?" Nadia called in panic from the top of the castle. Then she disappeared from sight.

Within a few minutes she was back, wearing Great-Hope's helmet low over her eyes. She shouted down angrily at the King's soldiers to go away. Then her friends who didn't know and love the King's Son joined in by telling the soldiers to leave Nadia alone, for she didn't need them bothering her.

Max and his friends with the flags and banners sensibly decided not to get into fights and heated arguments. So they hurried to Mount Freedom, all the time calling out to the King's Son to help Nadia. I was surprised to see that as they called to the King's Son, they seemed to be at peace, trusting in his strength, not in their own.

Around Castle Nadia there was anything but peace. The Magnificent Great-Hopes was not only still alive, he was running around crazily. From a storeroom at the back of the castle he handed armour to Nadia's friends. I'd seen it all before in the town of Mansoul: the helmet of Hope, the breastplate to harden and protect the heart from feeling the love of the King's Son, and the shield of Unbelief to catch the King's words and dash them to the ground. Then there was the sword shaped like a tongue with its end on fire to speak evil – not to be confused with the King's Sword I told you about just now – and finally the shield for the mouth, which had to be worn tightly to prevent the wearer calling out to the King's Son for help.

Everyone put on the armour eagerly, calling up to Nadia, who was still on top of her castle, that they'd defend her to the end.

Choosing sat in pain on the grass outside the castle door, shaking his head sadly. Fragments of rock from the catapults had badly wounded his skinny legs, so he was unable to move around to give encouragement to his companions. However, in spite of them wearing Great-Hope's armour, one thing was obvious – Nadia's friends were losing the battle.

By evening Nadia's friends collapsed in exhaustion, no longer having the will to fight for Nadia. A shout went up from the top of the castle. It was Nadia, telling them that the King's Son was standing by the white flag on Mount Freedom. Slowly and painfully her friends stood up, obviously wondering what the flag meant.

No one seemed to notice us as we swooped over the castle and joined the King's warriors on Mount Freedom. There we found Max and his friends, sitting with the King's Son who was writing a message for Nadia.

My dear Nadia, I wish you no harm. I have come to claim you as my own, to forgive you, and to make you new. Receive me now into your castle, and you will be mine and fly my flag.

The King's Son gave Max the task of delivering the message. After receiving a blessing, Max took it in his hand and made his way to Castle Nadia. Standing by the door he read the message aloud. Great-Hopes was back in his so-called palace behind the castle by this time, and realised too late what was happening. He hurried to the castle door, but not before everyone had heard what the King's Son had to say.

Great-Hopes pushed Max out of the way and called up to Nadia who was leaning out of a window with a puzzled look on her face. "If you want to change your ways," Great-Hopes shouted, "you don't need to ask the King's Son for help. *I* can help you live a life that will please him."

Choosing, who was sitting on the grass still bandaging his bony legs, turned to Great-Hopes. "I have heard the message," he told Great-Hopes. "The King's Son says he must come *into* the castle."

I was astonished to hear Choosing helping the King's Son. Talora looked equally surprised.

Great-Hopes seemed to be hiding his anger well. He smiled up at Nadia. "Just a matter of words," he called. "It is not necessary to carry out the instructions *exactly*. Trust me, I will make sure the King's Son is satisfied with your behaviour."

Great-Hopes hurried back to his hovel and returned with an armful of spears. He hurled these at Max and his friends, but they had already put on the gleaming armour supplied by the King's Son. The King's Helmets, Breastplates and Shields gave them all the defence they needed.

"To war, to war!" Great-Hopes screamed to Nadia. "Do not surrender now. If you do, you will look foolish in front of your friends, and regret it to the end of your days!"

CHAPTER 23

Escape

As the not-very-Magnificent Great-Hopes fled to the filthy shed he called his palace, the King's Son ordered Max and his friends to gather round.

"The battle is not over yet," he told them. "There are two men in a dungeon, and I have to set them free."

Unfortunately Max and his friends were unable to find the way in to rescue Conscience and Understanding. I wanted to help, but all I could see were brambles and nettles where I was sure the metal cover to the dungeon had been. Great-Hopes must have performed some sort of trick to confuse anyone wanting to mount a rescue.

That was when I remembered how I'd escaped from the dungeon with Talora, by squeezing through the narrow passage. "We'll help you rescue them," I said. "There's a ventilation tunnel."

"Let *me* go," Max said.

How could I explain that the rescuer needed to fly up to the metal cover to bang on it from the inside, without giving ourselves away? "We know the way," was all I said.

I went first, and Talora squeezed after me into the darkness. It was dangerous, and certainly not exciting, for we had no idea if we would emerge in the right place. Maybe the tunnel divided into two along the way, and we'd take the wrong turning and become stuck for ever. I wondered what would happen if we couldn't get into the dungeon and signal where the cover was to Max and his friends who would be waiting outside. Maybe the King's Son would never be able to enter Castle Nadia.

When we reached the tightest spot, I stopped crawling and called back to Talora. "I can smell the prison. We're nearly there." I've already mentioned the smell – how disgusting it was. I can't even start to describe it. You'll just have to use your imagination – and then try and picture it ten times worse.

I went a short distance further, forcing my way between the dark slimy walls of the tunnel. A voice suddenly called out of the blackness ahead.

"Who are you?"

"This is Zephan again," I whispered, as I squeezed out of the ventilation hole. Well, you feel like whispering when you're on a dangerous mission in enemy territory. I thought I recognised the voice from our earlier visit. "Are you Understanding?"

"Understanding is my name," the frightened voice said.

"Then I have good news for you." I was glad to stand up and stretch. "The Son of the Lord God is at the door of Castle Nadia. He wants you two out of here."

"Do you think we would still be here if we could escape?" Conscience asked from the darkness.

Understanding crept over to me. "It is partly our fault," he explained. "Great-Hopes sealed the outside, but this place is of our own making. You cannot understand how a person could be so foolish as to make his own prison, but that is exactly what Conscience has done. This was once a wide hole that was quite shallow, but he has dug it deeper and deeper, piling up the earth at the sides so the shaft has become very deep and narrow. And now there is no way for us to escape."

"But why keep digging down?" Talora asked.

"Because Conscience has been behaving stupidly." Understanding sounded angry. "He is not to be trusted any longer. What hope is there for any of us now?"

"We've come to get you out," I said impatiently. "But we have to do it quickly."

"I do not see how," Understanding complained. "You have already tried to push the heavy cover aside, and we cannot escape through the tunnel."

"I'm going to fly up and shout," I explained. "There are people up there, but they can't find the cover. Great-Hopes has concealed it."

Talora said she'd stay below, to give me a bit more room. I flew up, my wings knocking heavily against the walls, but I got there in the end and clung onto the iron ring under the grating.

"I'm here! I'm here!" I shouted as loudly as I could. I just had to hope someone outside was close enough to hear me.

Then we heard scraping and scratching noises, and a voice shouted, "This is Max. If Conscience and Understanding want to escape from their prison, the King's Son says they have to call out to him. Tell them to do it now before it's too late."

I dropped down quickly to be with Conscience and Understanding. "You must trust the King's Son," I said, sensing some doubt in the long pause before either of them spoke.

"We have no other way of getting free," Understanding admitted reluctantly. "I will call out to the King's Son for help." But he stayed silent.

"Go on then, call," I urged.

"Help," Understanding called feebly. "Help."

Conscience joined in, and each time they called their voices became louder and stronger.

Suddenly I caught hold of the two men and pulled them to the side. "The cover is coming off."

Understanding and Conscience cried out in distress as the sunlight dazzled their eyes. The group above quickly lowered a rope ladder. As the two men emerged from their prison, some of Nadia's friends pushed Max away. When they saw the prisoners hiding their eyes, they turned to each other in alarm.

"The soldiers have blinded them," they told each other. "See, we knew something terrible would happen if Nadia talked to the King's Son. What hope is there for her now?"

"Nadia is doomed," a girl said. "I've just heard that Prejudice has been killed in the fighting."

"And Blindfold," a boy called.

"I think Hesitate is finished too," another added.

Choosing started shouting in front of the castle, and everyone hurried to see him calling out to Nadia's friends.

"I have checked on the dead and wounded," Choosing announced, in a surprisingly powerful voice. He'd bandaged his legs and was able to get around quite well now, although he moved slowly. I even thought he'd put on a little weight, and certainly his voice was stronger. "The only people who are dead are the some of Great-Hopes' companions from round the back of the castle. The King's Son is waiting on Mount Freedom for Nadia to invite him in." He turned to Nadia. "What reply shall I give him?"

"Tell him I claim the peace and forgiveness he offers," Nadia called from the doorway of her castle. "Tell him I want him as my King."

Choosing wrote a message begging the King's Son to forgive everything Nadia had ever done wrong, and to come immediately and make the castle his own. He gave it to a girl called Try-Hard, with instructions for her to hurry across to Mount

Freedom. In all the excitement we forgot that we shouldn't draw attention to ourselves by flying, so we launched ourselves into the air and were on Mount Freedom before Try-Hard arrived. This sounded good.

Try-Hard handed the paper to the King's Son, but the sun shining off his armour made her screw up her eyes as though she was unable to see clearly. She must have thought the King's Son turned away without reading the message, for she turned quickly and hurried back to the castle with bad news.

Choosing told Try-Hard she must try again. He wrote another message, but once more the shining armour dazzled Try-Hard. She returned to the castle to say that she believed that the message had still not been read.

"Let me take the message for you."

Everyone turned to see who had spoken. Young Good-Deeds made his way to the front again.

"I'm not afraid to see the King's Son," he boasted. "I know he turned me away once, but this time he will be pleased to see me."

Choosing nodded in agreement. "All right, you may go again."

But Conscience had now recovered from his time in prison, and he held out his hand to stop Good-Deeds going. "Don't be so foolish," he told Good-Deeds. "If the King's Son sees that Nadia relies on messengers such as you, he will think she doesn't really need him."

Nadia nodded thoughtfully. "Yes, Good-Deeds, as far as the King's Son is concerned, you're worthless." She turned to Conscience. "So who do we send?"

"Send Tears," Conscience told her.

Nadia sighed, but looked calmer than she had been for days. "Yes, I want to send Tears."

CHAPTER 24

Sending Tears

Choosing stood on tiptoe and looked around. He didn't have to look far to see Tears sitting on the grass, her head resting in her hands. She looked up with a sad smile and said, yes, perhaps she should be the one to go.

No one seemed to have noticed us flying backwards and forwards between Castle Nadia and Mount Freedom, so Talora flew with me as we followed Tears across the valley to Mount Freedom where the King's Son stood watching the castle.

"Please don't be angry with Nadia for sending messengers to you so often," Tears said, looking at the ground. "If you could only show her that you're ready to listen …" She stopped, unable to speak for the tears streaming down her face.

The King's Son put his hands on Tears' shoulder. "Tell me," he said, "where is Nadia's young friend Good-Deeds? I expected him to come again."

"Nadia wouldn't allow him to come," Tears explained. "She said Good-Deeds isn't worthy. And neither am I worthy," Tears added quickly, "but Nadia thought you might listen to me asking for mercy and forgiveness."

"Go back to the castle," the King's Son replied.

Tears began to turn away.

"Don't go so quickly, because I have a message for Nadia," the King's Son said, making Tears turn back. "Tell her I am pleased she has sent you, but now she must come herself. I want no fine clothes to impress me. She is to come here to meet me now, dressed just as she is. And she is not to bring Good-Deeds or Try-Hard, or any of their companions."

I noticed that the King's Son had to turn away as he spoke, to hide the sadness in his own eyes, while Tears went back to the castle looking dejected.

"Well?" Nadia asked as soon as Tears came back. She stood in front of her castle, the door behind her slightly open.

"You have to meet the King's Son," Tears explained.

Nadia gasped in horror. She said she wasn't wearing her best clothes, and as she looked at them they seemed to get more soiled. She began to cry. "I can't go yet. I have to change into something cleaner."

"No," Tears told her. "The King's Son wants to meet you now, dressed just as you are."

Nadia started to brush her clothes down, but it was a hopeless task. "I can't go like *this*," she protested.

"Dressed just as you are, is what the King's Son said," Tears repeated. "And you cannot take Good-Deeds or Try-Hard with you, or any of their companions."

For a moment Nadia hesitated, and I was expecting her to storm back inside her castle and slam the door. But no, she'd made up her mind and began to cross to the camp on Mount Freedom where the King's Son ... But he was no longer there. He was hurrying over to greet Nadia. And when I say hurrying, it was as though one moment the King's Son was on Mount Freedom, and within an eye-blink he was here with Nadia.

"Tell me, Nadia, what do you want me to do?" the King's Son asked.

Tears stood close to them both.

"I have come because you called me," Nadia said.

The King's Son looked at her. "You had Great-Hopes and Good-Deeds. And what about Try-Hard? Were you not content with them?"

Nadia knelt down with Tears. "I was, because I had no idea there was a better way," she said quietly.

"And now you want me as your King?"

"I do," Nadia whispered.

Tears nodded her head in agreement, then slipped away leaving Nadia alone with the King's Son. Nadia dried her eyes and stood up. "I accept you as my King," she cried out happily. "Come into my castle and be my King for ever."

The King's Son waited for Nadia to lift the heavy latch. Then, in his armour of gleaming gold he entered with her. Only a few of Nadia's friends had stayed to watch.

"Whatever's going to happen now?" I heard a girl whisper. "I think Nadia's gone mad."

"The King's Son may not have come in peace," one of the boys said.

"I don't think he really wants Nadia to be his friend," another boy whispered. "It's a trick, to punish her. Nadia is making a big mistake."

Of course I wanted to see what was going on inside Castle Nadia. The Lord God had said we couldn't enter these castles, but he had told us we could watch and listen. And I could see that one of Nadia's windows was wide. The problem was that the window was high up, but we had an easy way round that. We spread our wings and took off. My wings felt more bruised and sore as time went on. It must have been squeezing through that narrow tunnel that did it, but they worked well enough.

As we perched on the ledge of the open window we could

hear Nadia talking to the King's Son. "Please come in peace," she said quietly. "I don't want to fight you any more."

We saw the King's Son take Nadia by the arm and go out with her through the castle door, never saying a word.

"Where are they going," Talora asked, as we flew high above the castle. "Is the King's Son leaving?"

"I think he's taking Nadia to find the Magnificent Great-Hopes. Yes, he's stopped at the door of Great-Hopes' fleapit."

I jumped as a trumpet blast sounded over the castle, and everyone fell to their knees. As the King's Son came to Great-Hopes' door he touched it, and it crumbled into a pile of dust. Great-Hopes had dressed himself in armour, but the warrior angels dragged him out of the ruins and ripped it off. Great-Hopes stood there in his shabby underwear, no longer magnificent.

When he saw the King's Son, Great-Hopes fell to his knees and begged for mercy. And the more he begged, the smaller he seemed to grow, until he looked like nothing compared to the Son of the Creator King, the Lord God of the Universe. But as Nadia turned round to see what her friends were thinking, Great-Hopes broke free and raced down the hill.

If this were all that happened, it would be amazing. But there was much more. Many of Nadia's friends, who had come to help her fight the King's Son, knelt down and begged for forgiveness too. The King's Son gave them peace and pardon, and welcomed them into his family.

"You are children of the Lord God now," he told them. "You are my brothers and my sisters."

As the King's Son led Nadia back into her castle, from the sky came the sound of angels singing. The most beautiful singing they'd ever heard – so Nadia's new friends said. Across the hills and valleys we heard singing coming from other castles, and as night fell there was much joy in Heaven and on Earth.

I don't want to spoil things for you, but I had an uncomfortable feeling that all was not well. And, as we will see, I was right.

CHAPTER 25

Peace

The singing and music went on late into the night, making people in nearby castles turn sleeplessly in their beds. As Talora walked around with me, we could hear some of Nadia's friends who had stayed by the castle discussing what had happened. One of them worried whether the King's Son had really come in peace. Another thought maybe Nadia and her friends who had welcomed the Lord God would be asked to make too many changes, and not want to bother with them anymore.

The next morning the sun rose in a clear blue sky. I even remarked on the colour to Talora, remembering how this journey to Earth had started with a discussion on Eltor about whether a sky could really be blue.

In the early sunlight, the King's Son hugged Nadia and her friends – Nadia now called them her special friends – who had given themselves to him, and handed them the richest white robes to wear.

"These are royal robes," the King's Son explained. "They are made of the finest white linen."

When Nadia knew for sure that the King's Son had come in peace, and had indeed forgiven her, she put on her robe and leapt and danced about, praising him.

In the end, Nadia became so overwhelmed with emotion that the King's Son had to hold her tightly in his arms. Then, with tears flooding down her cheeks, she knelt. A strange thing happened. The sky was still clear blue, but a gentle rain started to fall. I took hold of Talora's hand. We didn't feel the need to shelter, because the rain was so soft. It flowed down the walls and windows of Nadia's castle, and the castles of her special friends, washing them clean. I felt sure the Lord God had sent the cleansing rain to give them a clearer view of his Kingdom across the River.

The special friends ran back to their own castles to celebrate their new commitment to the King's Son, while I stayed with Talora outside Castle Nadia. As the rain stopped, a white dove flew down and settled on top of the castle walls.

The King's Son pointed to it. "Look, Nadia," he said, "it is a sign that the Holy Spirit has come to live with you. My Father, the Holy Spirit and I are one. It is hard for you to understand, but you can trust me that it is so."

Talora nudged me. "The King's Son is right, Zephan. People who belong to the King believe it, but they can never understand it properly."

"I'm not surprised," I said. "They've not been to Heaven yet."

The King's Son pointed again to the dove and, as Nadia watched, a flag appeared with a dove emblazoned on it. This time it was easy to see that this was a genuine flag, not a homemade copy.

"There are some castles around that will be pleased to see this flag," the King's Son told Nadia. "But the owners of many castles will make fun of you."

A group appeared, all dressed in white linen robes. Among them were Max and his friends, and Nadia's special friends who had turned to the King's Son for forgiveness. It struck me that this was a way in which Talora and I were allowed to see them. To each other, they probably seemed to be dressed in jeans and other casual clothes. The more I thought about it, the more I could see that this must be how the King's Son saw all his followers. The royal robes were his gift, white robes covering them with love and forgiveness.

The celebrations lasted throughout the day. The King's Son walked around, meeting everyone carrying a banner. When it was evening he stood outside the door of Castle Nadia, and raised his hands to Nadia and her friends.

"Be at peace," he told them. "It is time for you to get some rest. Tomorrow I will tell you the plans I have for you." He turned to Nadia and pointed to Max and the crowd holding banners. "Everyone here is your friend, Nadia. Keep close to them, and strengthen each other in your faith."

The others may have felt ready for rest, but clearly Nadia didn't. She ran to the top of her castle and picked up a trumpet. I learnt later that each owner has a trumpet they can blow in times of happiness. Nadia blew hers so loudly, and made such beautiful music, that she disturbed many of the people in neighbouring castles, who grumbled at what they called unnecessary excitement.

Other people climbed onto the roofs of their castles and put out huge banners of welcome to the King's Son, wanting the whole world to know that the Son of the Lord God had rescued them and forgiven them.

By the time Nadia was finally at rest, Talora wanted to sit down with me and talk about everything that had happened since coming here. As we sat in the darkness, someone slipped past. For a moment I felt a chill of unease. It was difficult to see clearly, but he was overweight and looked like . . .

"What's the matter?" Talora asked.

"I saw … No, it can't have been."

"Tell me who you think it was," Talora insisted.

"You remember Won't-Believe in Mansoul? A big man. He was holding the Ear Gate shut."

"You've seen him here?"

"He just ran past. Come on, let's use our wings and follow him. I want to see where he's going. Don't talk any more."

As we flew above the running figure, I could see that it was indeed Won't-Believe. We stayed with him as he puffed his way up Shadow Hill, muttering to himself that he had to find his old friend Diabolus. He entered the Shadowed Wood, crashing past the sickly trees until he reached a cave underneath a high rock.

We landed quickly and started to walk cautiously. The ground underfoot was soft and slippery with moss, and the lower branches of the trees reached out as we pushed past, snapping at our arms and legs like greedy fingers.

I began to feel anxious, for I could detect great evil in the air. A shadow angel stood guard at the mouth of the cave. This definitely was not a safe place for ordinary angels like us. Even so, I wanted to know what was happening inside. Trusting the Lord God to keep us safe, we found a gap between the rocks at the entrance where we could hide, and hear and see everything inside. Holding our noses against the stench, we listened in horror.

Diabolus himself was there. He sounded furious as Won't-Believe described what had happened. Then he leapt to his feet. "Do you mean to say some of my friends at Castle Nadia have been *killed*?" he stormed.

Won't-Believe replied that it definitely looked that way.

"Very well," Diabolus said, calming down just a little, "I am going now, and you will wait here patiently. Nadia may think her castle is strong and easy to defend, but the time will come when she will forget about the King's Son and all he has done for her. She will soon wonder if she has been forgiven, and even doubt that there really is a Creator God who cares for her. And when that happens, and it surely will, you must let me know at once."

CHAPTER 26

The Enemy

We had not tried to stop Won't-Believe on his way to the cave. This was something I now regretted, although I think the King's Son would have told us to do it if he wanted Won't-Believe stopped. Anyway, I could see that this creature was going to cause a lot of trouble.

The next morning I went with Talora to help Nadia and the Lord God's warrior angels capture four of these enemies of the King who were still hiding close to her castle. The soldiers put them in chains and brought them to the front of the castle where the King's Son said they must stand trial.

Nadia's new friends, a large group carrying white banners, were already there, offering Nadia support. Max was there too with his friends. The prisoners on trial were Hate, Anger, Greed and Dishonesty. Each was charged with helping turn Nadia against the Lord God.

The prisoners tried to defend their deeds, but when the King's Son asked Nadia for her verdict she declared all of them guilty – and everyone cheered loudly.

"What happens now?" I asked, as soon as the last prisoner had been convicted.

"Ssssh," Talora whispered. "We mustn't talk during the trial."

The King's Son stood up. "Nadia," he said, "you have found these prisoners guilty. What is your wish that I should do with them?"

"Put them to death," she said quietly.

The King's Son nodded. "I will help you deal with them."

I watched the prisoners tremble with fear when they heard this, but Nadia showed no pity. This was certainly not the hesitant Nadia who'd been running around in panic yesterday, unable to decide what to do. The King's Son handed Nadia a Sword with a flashing blade.

"I don't think I'm going to like this," Talora said, turning away.

The King's Son noticed Talora standing with me, and came across. "There is nothing to fear," he assured her. "These prisoners are companions of Diabolus, my enemy. It is right for Nadia to use my Sword to destroy them."

Talora turned back to see what was happening, but too late. All four creatures lay dead on the ground, and Nadia was wiping the Sword on the grass. No one seemed upset by this. In fact, another loud cheer went up from Nadia's new friends. I could see some words engraved on the blade of the Sword in shimmering letters, but we were too far away to read them.

"Do not worry," the King's Son said. "They will be buried out of sight. Tell me, Talora, are you glad for Nadia, or are you sorry for the prisoners?"

Talora smiled. "Glad for Nadia of course. Yes, I was wrong to feel pity for the prisoners. But some of them escaped last night."

The King's Son nodded. "There are many who have escaped, but at the moment Nadia is feeling pleased that these companions of Diabolus have been dealt with."

"I was wondering about the Shadowed Wood," I said.

"There's a cave there where Won't-Believe and others are hiding."

"What do you have in mind, Zephan?"

"I thought that … well … that we could go there and kill Won't-Believe – if you want us to."

The King's Son shook his head. "I have to wait for Nadia to ask before I can do anything," he explained. "Today she wants me to rebuild the castle. She may think it is in a good position, but we need to make it strong and well defended against my enemy. I have appointed Understanding to lend a hand, and I am appointing Knowledge to be the Keeper of Wisdom. I am sure you remember Knowledge from Mansoul."

"I thought Conscience would get that job," I said in surprise, for I could remember both of them in Mansoul. No, that's not quite right. It seemed to me that there were lots of these creatures sharing the same names. Maybe each castle had a set, some whispering good thoughts, some whispering bad.

"You are right," the King's Son replied. "Conscience should be an excellent choice, but he has suffered in that dreadful dungeon and may not be too reliable at present. Knowledge is a good friend of mine, and understands what I want for Nadia."

That afternoon, outside the castle door, a healthy-looking Choosing stood with Nadia as she apologised for her past mistakes. The King's Son assured Nadia yet again that he had given her a full pardon. Nadia's new friends clapped loudly, for Choosing was seen as the one who had finally helped invite the King's Son into the castle.

"Choosing, you ought to be the Keeper of the Door for Nadia," a friend who was holding a white banner called out, and the others joined in.

Nadia smiled. "Yes, Choosing, be the Keeper of the Door."

Choosing said he'd be pleased to agree to the position, and

Nadia's new friends arranged a party for that evening, with tables laid out in front of the castle. They invited the King's Son as guest of honour. When he accepted the invitation, he told Nadia and her friends to sit down on the grass. Nadia told Max and his friends they would be welcome too.

"Nadia, my own castle," the King's Son said, "in the name of my Father I have granted you free, full and everlasting forgiveness for all the wrong you have done against me, against my Father and against the Holy Spirit, against your family, your friends, your neighbours, and against yourself. I have already let you use this Sword, and now I want you to keep it."

I stood on tiptoe to see the King's Son hand Nadia not a Sword, but a copy of the Lord God's Holy Book, the Bible.

"This is a powerful weapon," the King's Son explained. "It is a Sword that will protect you, a Light that will guide you in the right way, and Words that will instruct and comfort you. You may talk with me whenever you wish, and one day my angels will bring you to live with me around my Father's throne."

Nadia's new friends interrupted the speech by cheering loudly, shouting praises to the King's Son.

Talora touched my arm. "I'd like to help take Nadia to Heaven when the time comes," she whispered.

No one can keep a secret from the King's Son. He caught Talora's eye, smiled and nodded. Waiting until the praise had died away he spoke again, sounding serious. "Nadia and friends, Great-Hopes dug many hiding places around the walls of your castles while he was in charge, because he knew the day was coming when I would attack. I am giving you orders to go out every day and destroy the enemy. Wear the armour I am giving you, and deal with the enemy with your Swords – but never, ever go into battle without me."

When they heard this, Nadia and her new friends waved

their Swords in the air, and again I could see the flash of letters on the blades, for the Books had again become Swords.

"I want you to visit other castles in the area," the King's Son continued. "Some of them, like Castle Max, fly my flag. Talk with the people who live there about me. Some castles are in the hands of the enemy. If the people will listen, tell them what I have done for you – and what I want to do for them. And remember, I am with you always, to give you peace."

Then the King's Son took Nadia inside and showed her a secret room in the heart of her castle. "In this room," he explained, "the Holy Spirit has now come to live. He will give you grace and strength."

Nadia was so glad to know the Holy Spirit was living with her that she cried out again with praise. She said the Holy Spirit looked so like the King's Son that he must be the same person. The next moment she said she could tell he was the Creator God himself come to live in her castle.

The King's Son looked at us and smiled, for he knew we understood how One can be Three, and Three can be One. Then he spoke to Nadia again. "The Holy Spirit will teach you. He has brought many useful gifts, but you must ask him for them. Love him as you love me."

Nadia's new friends who were busy laying the tables outside the castle cheered once more, and I found myself caught up in the praise offered to the Lord God, the Creator. Talora looked overjoyed.

But part of me still felt uneasy.

CHAPTER 27

The Cave

I felt there was trouble brewing from the creatures living among the unhealthy trees on Shadow Hill. As soon as the party was underway, I suggested to Talora that she stayed where she was, and I'd fly to the cave where Won't-Believe had run last night.

Already it was getting dark, but the group at the party with the King's Son and Max outside Castle Nadia was likely to stay there well into the night, celebrating by the light of burning torches. After leaving the castle I reached Shadow Hill and saw the companions of Diabolus below me, slipping through the sickly trees like snakes.

I flew back to Talora, who looked at me in surprise. "Your face has gone pale," she said. "Is it the torchlight?"

I assured her it wasn't.

"Then what's the matter?"

"There's a terrible evil out there."

Talora shook her head. "While you were gone, I've been watching everyone dancing in their white robes. What could possibly be the matter?"

I held onto her arm. "Won't-Believe and his gang are moving in the wood."

"Are they coming this way?"

I shrugged my shoulders – well, my wings really. "They may

be. I didn't wait to see."

Talora laughed. "You're being foolish," she insisted. "They won't be coming here. This is the happiest day I have ever known. It reminds me of times around the throne of the Lord God – but even better, because the King's Son has rescued Nadia and her friends. And now they are all part of one big family."

I pulled Talora away from the tables. "Stand still," I told her. "Now, do you feel anything bad?"

Talora said nothing, and shook her head.

"Remember when we first arrived on Earth, Talora, and the shadow angels came looking for us?"

Talora closed her eyes and turned her head away from the castle wall. "Yes," she said at last. "Yes, Zephan, I think you're right. I can sense the enemy now."

"That means they're getting closer. So what are we going to do?"

The answer to my question came from the far end of the tables in front of the castle. The King's Son looked up and caught sight of me talking to Talora. The smile faded from his face as he understood what was in our minds. He called us over, and without anyone else hearing told us to go and seek out the enemy and then report back.

The celebrations continued as we stood up to leave, the exciting atmosphere helped by the flare of a hundred burning torches.

"I'm a bit scared," Talora admitted. "Where are we going first?"

"Let's fly up high above the castle," I suggested. "I know it's dark, but there's a moon. We may be able to see what's happening from up there."

"Perhaps the companions of Diabolus aren't coming here

after all." Not that Talora sounded as though she believed it.

The moon went behind a thick cloud, so no matter how high we flew we could see nothing but deep shadows below.

"Let's go down and listen," Talora suggested.

Back on the ground we stood still and listened carefully. A sound like whispering came from the long grass growing along the foot of the castle walls, but we decided it was just the breeze.

"I'm going to fly to the Shadowed Wood for another look," I said at last. "The enemy may still be there." I have to admit I was getting nervous, even though I wanted to do something to help. "You don't have to come with me."

Talora held onto my arm. "We'll go together. And we'll go in the name of the Lord God."

"You're right," I said. "But we may still get injured."

Talora moved ahead of me. "The Lord God has sent us here to do his work, so I'm not afraid of what the enemy does to me."

Talora made me feel extra bold. We swooped over the banqueting tables and the flaring torches, then rose high in the air. A few minutes later, as the moon came out from a gap in the clouds, we landed on Shadow Hill.

For a moment I felt anxious as the moon disappeared again and the darkness closed in around us. Cautiously, I led the way between the trees with the clutching branches.

"Zephan," Talora asked, "are you just a bit scared?"

"A bit. I'm remembering what you said. The Lord God is with us." But I could no longer feel the Creator's presence. I could trust him though – trust his promise to be here.

"Well?" Talora asked.

I shrugged. "The enemy is close. I just know it. Look, look over there. See that light?"

As we crept through the spindly trees, getting closer to the middle of the Shadowed Wood, the twisted branches tried to wrap themselves round our legs like evil claws, and we had to kick them away. It was as though they knew who we were. A dim glow came from the low entrance to the cave where Won't-Believe had run last night.

"Someone's still in there," Talora whispered.

"Go quietly," I warned, not liking this one little bit. "There may be a sentry on guard."

Do angels get scared easily? Not usually, but we know serious danger when we come across it – and this felt like serious danger.

For several minutes we stood and listened. No movement came from inside the cave. We crept closer on the damp ground, but stopped as soon as we heard voices.

"How about this disguise?" we heard someone ask. "Nadia knows what I look like, but she won't recognise me now. She'll think I'm one of her new friends."

Another creature laughed. "You look wonderful."

I moved closer to the cave. In the flickering firelight I could see several companions of Diabolus, but the smoke inside was thick. I could just make out Self-Pleasing wearing old clothes. He must have been the one boasting about his disguise.

And then I recognised Won't-Believe. I stepped back in alarm, treading on a stick. It snapped with a sharp noise. Inside the cave everyone stopped talking.

"Quick, Talora, we have to get away!"

But we were too late. The companions of Diabolus rushed out and seized us.

"Two spies, nicely caught before they can report back." Self-Pleasing looked at us with burning hatred in his eyes. "So nearly did we fail in our plan, but now ... now nothing can stand in our way!"

CHAPTER 28

A Disguise

The companions of Diabolus tied us up tightly, very tightly, and I'm sure they went out of their way to hurt us as they tugged at the knots. I'm not feeling sorry for myself, or for Talora – we knew what to expect – but I think it worth mentioning here that it's not nice to fall into the clutches of these creatures. Having hit us about our heads, they threw us into the back of the cave. That was when I knew there was nothing we could do to stop Self-Pleasing from visiting Nadia.

Self-Pleasing laughed. "See, you two pretty ones, don't you think I look handsome?"

"All I can think was that you make me want to be sick," Talora said.

"What makes you suppose Nadia will accept *you* as one of her new friends?" I asked, still feeling bold in spite of the pain from the tight cords. "You *look* like a friend of Diabolus, and nothing else!"

"You say that because you angels don't understand how it is with people," Self-Pleasing sneered. "Soon Nadia will want to be friends with us again. Isn't that so, Won't-Believe?" He turned to his companion and they both laughed.

I felt angry. "You saw what Nadia did to some of you with the King's Sword. Do you really think *you* can escape from the

King's Son?"

"We will take more care not to be noticed this time," Won't-Believe told us. He sounded confident, and the shadow from his large body seemed to make the cave darker.

I shook my head. These creatures were certainly making a nuisance of themselves right now. "The King's Son has already warned Nadia and her friends about enemies like you."

"You think Nadia is on the look-out for us?" Won't-Believe snapped. "She's forgotten we even exist."

The creatures looked at each other.

Won't-Believe smiled. "Self-Pleasing is right." Then he laughed. "It is clear *you* do not know much about the ways of Nadia and her friends!"

"And perhaps *you* do not know how much the King's Son loves them!" Talora retorted, which sounded to me an extremely good answer. I wished I'd thought of it myself.

The night was long and cold in the back of the cave. I'm an angel, so why didn't I slip out through the ropes, untie Talora, and fly back to Castle Nadia to warn the King's Son that the enemy was on the way? Well, angels can't do magic things, and no matter how hard I tried to escape, Self-Pleasing and Won't-Believe had tied us up too well.

I called out to the Lord God, asking him not to let these creatures find Nadia. But like last night, I got no sense of the presence of the King's Son. Something strange was happening. It seemed as though his enemies had become too powerful. Maybe we had to be patient, for surely the King's Son knew what was happening here, and had some rescue in mind for us – as well as for Nadia and her new friends.

Next morning Self-Pleasing put on his disguise. Saying goodbye to his companions, he told them he was going to Castle Nadia to wait. He was confident Choosing would give his usual permission for Nadia to come out when the sun rose over the distant hills. If there were enough of Nadia's new friends about, Self-Pleasing said he would probably be able to slip amongst them and cause problems. However, I knew that Conscience would be there with Choosing, so they would help protect Nadia if they recognised Self–Pleasing. Wouldn't they?

A few minutes later I heard the answer for myself, even though we were tied up in the back of the cave in the Shadowed Wood.

"Be on your way!" Conscience's thunderous voice sounded clear, even at this distance. Well, he'd certainly recovered rapidly since we helped him escape from Great-Hopes' prison. "You are no friend of Nadia," he shouted. "Where is your white robe?"

A few minutes later Self-Pleasing was back at the cave, breathless, bruised and scratched from where he must have fallen running back up Shadow Hill.

"You fool!" Won't-Believe shouted at him as he staggered into the cave. "Why have you come back *here*? Maybe someone has followed you. Better they kill *you* than us!"

Self-Pleasing had gashed his leg when he fell, and he was busy tying an old rag round it to stop the bleeding. "I didn't have the right clothes," he explained in embarrassment.

"Fantastic!" Won't-Believe yelled. "Now everyone knows we're living in this cave in the Shadowed Wood!"

"No, no," Self-Pleasing said quickly. "You needn't worry. Nobody followed me. I was turning round all the time to check. That's why I kept falling over. The King's Son has dressed Nadia and her friends in robes of the purest white. I didn't stand a chance in these old things. Do we have anything white I can wear?"

"White?" Talora laughed. "Where would someone like you

find anything white round here?"

"*Silence!*" Self-Pleasing roared. "When we are out to deceive a castle, we can *appear* to be dressed in white. Wait until tomorrow morning, then you'll understand how clever we are."

I decided to keep still and save my strength for later, when we might get a chance to escape. I have to say that the day, and then the night, passed extremely slowly. It was an uncomfortable time for us.

As the sun rose the next morning and lit up the entrance to the cave, we watched Self-Pleasing put a long, white robe over his dirty clothing. White? No, it wasn't particularly white, and I couldn't think it would deceive Nadia.

"A thousand curses on the sun," Self-Pleasing said, looking out of the cave and shaking his fist. "I must wait for a darker day. Then perhaps Nadia and her friends will receive me gladly."

Well, although it was unpleasant being tied up, I took some comfort from knowing that these creatures would be leaving Nadia and her new friends alone for a time. However, as the night and then the next day passed, and then the next night and next day, I began to feel tired. Angels don't need to eat, so a lack of food wasn't the problem. Of course, we can eat when we're mixing with people on Earth, and have done so on several famous occasions; but when we're tied up in a dark cave, food is neither here nor there. And it certainly wasn't here. Even if it had been, we wouldn't have touched the sort of stuff these creatures devoured.

Every morning Self-Pleasing went out to see if it was the right sort of weather to join Nadia and her friends. Always he returned frustrated.

"Will they *never* tire of worshiping their King?" he complained. "I can't keep these clothes white much longer."

Talora laughed again. "That robe is even dirtier than the first time you wore it – and it was filthy then."

"Ssssh!" Won't-Believe hissed. "You two will soon see how powerful the companions of Diabolus are!"

One day, Self-Pleasing thought the weather was right and he went out. An hour passed, then another. By late afternoon he still hadn't returned. The sun set. Darkness came over the whole countryside.

"There!" Won't-Believe gloated. "Nadia and her new friends have accepted Self-Pleasing!"

"Perhaps he's been captured, and killed with the King's Sword," Talora suggested.

Won't-Believe didn't like to hear such an idea. "Do you think we're *stupid?*" he asked.

"No," Talora said. "We know you are cunning and evil, but you must surely know that the Son of the Lord God is far, far greater than you."

At the mention of the Lord God's name, Won't-Believe set on us and kept beating us with a heavy stick until we both fell unconscious.

I drifted in and out of wakefulness, on one occasion noticing that the trees of the Shadowed Wood looked more dead than usual, the branches even more bare, and covered in white stuff I guessed was snow. The conspirators always stayed huddled together as though waiting for someone.

"Winter," I told myself. I knew Earth would have seasons, just like Eltor, but we'd only been here a short time and had never seen winter. But even as I watched, the snow melted and the sun shone higher in the sky. Time was passing in a way that only angels know.

"Look, shadow angels!" Talora spoke to me in alarm. "They must have arrived when we were unconscious."

That brought me fully awake. The sun was well up in the sky, and the cave entrance was bright. The inside of the cave, however, seemed more depressing than ever.

"We must be very quiet," I whispered, blinking and shaking my head to clear my thoughts. "Do they know we're here?"

The companions of Diabolus and the shadow angels were talking in a large circle. As far as I could see, not one of them was looking in our direction.

Talora raised her head. "Perhaps they saw us when they arrived, but I've been in a dream-world since Won't-Believe beat us up."

"Me too. I wonder how long they've been here. It must be months."

Talora gasped. "Look, Zephan, I can see Self-Pleasing. He's talking to the shadow angels. I wonder why he's come back. I *must* hear what they're talking about. I think I can roll over towards them."

"Be careful," I warned. "Oh, Talora, please be ever so careful."

CHAPTER 29

Shadow Angels

While Talora rolled her way slowly across the floor of the cave, neither the shadow angels nor Self-Pleasing's gang of deceivers took any notice. I think they were too excited by their plotting to look anywhere but at each other.

"What were they saying?" I asked impatiently, as soon as Talora came back to me.

She had bad news. "Nadia made friends with Self-Pleasing. It seems none of her new friends have realised he's a friend of Diabolus. Nadia is thinking of making him her leader when he returns. If only we could escape and warn her!"

I pointed outside the cave where it was now springtime, but a very poor springtime here in the Shadowed Wood. "I have an idea."

In spite of trusting the King's Son to rescue us, it seemed to me that he had left us here for a very long time. Not far from me I spotted a rusty sword that must belong to one of the shadow angels.

"Talora, you can roll about the cave quite well now. See that old sword by that rock? Roll over and feel if the blade is sharp enough to cut your ropes. And be careful no one sees you."

The shadow angels and the companions of Diabolus were still deep in conversation, and never once glanced in our direction. Within a few minutes Talora had cut through her cords, but the sword was too heavy to move.

"Now that my hands and feet are free I can come over and untie you," she whispered.

"Be quick," I said. "The shadow angels have started singing. I think they're getting ready to leave."

Talora nodded. "I heard one of them say they have to report to Diabolus. Perhaps I'd better lie down and pretend to be tied up."

"No," I insisted, "untie me now. We need to get out of here fast."

Talora untied me before the shadow angels were into the second verse of a song of victory. I spoke urgently to her. "They're so full of their singing they've closed their eyes. Be very quiet, and we'll creep past them."

As quietly as giskos – or should I say mice – we slipped past the group of conspirators and into the daylight. A team of dirty horses, tethered outside the cave, snorted in alarm as we appeared, pushing at us, trying to stop our escape.

The shadow angels ran out of the cave.

"Keep with me, Talora. We can get to Castle Nadia if we're quick!"

By the time the shadow angels had sorted themselves out and jumped on their horses, Talora and I were out of the trees and able to spread our wings. I looked back at Shadow Hill. The shadow angels sat in a row on their horses, glaring at us but not coming any closer. Maybe they needed instructions from Diabolus.

Just before we reached Castle Nadia we dropped to the grass and started to walk. Weeds and brambles grew every-where around the castle walls.

I don't think any of Nadia's friends realised it, but while

some of them were still in their white robes, others were back in their ordinary clothes. Not that the white robes looked very special after all this time. I knew that the Lord God has given angels special vision to see these robes that are invisible to humans, and there are times when what we see comes as a real surprise. Some of the most holy-looking people seem to be wearing old rags, while other – very ordinary – followers of the Lord God shine brightly.

Choosing had definitely lost weight again in the few months we'd been away. He could see our white cloaks, and he started to laugh. "Why, you two have kept yourselves amazingly clean!" he called. "Where have you been?"

"Trapped in a cave," I said, and Choosing looked puzzled.

He didn't try to stop us mixing with Nadia's friends. I was going to say Nadia's new friends, but I recognised many of her old ones in the group. It was only right that Nadia had all sorts of friends, but some of these made me uneasy because she seemed to be trying to copy them.

The shadow angels now started to advance on horseback, but suddenly turned and rode back into the Shadowed Wood. I wondered why. Nadia's friends paused and listened intently. Aware that something was making them feel uncomfortable, they looked alarmed. But never once did any of them call out to the King's Son for help.

"Talora! Zephan!"

We looked round in surprise at hearing the voice of the King's Son.

"Things have been dangerous for both of you."

"Where are you?" I asked.

"I am over here." The voice came from the shelter of a high rock.

With Talora close behind me, we ran over.

"Nadia is very precious to me," the King's Son said sorrowfully, "but I know she would no longer recognise me if she saw me."

We knelt as the gentle figure appeared before us. Now I knew why the shadow angels had fled. "We wanted to warn you," I blurted out, "but we got caught. Ages ago."

The King's Son came close. "Do you think I did not know? Oh, Zephan and Talora, I have been watching over you every minute," he said. "I am sorry you got hurt, but I could not let you escape until you learned more about the ways in which my enemy works. You must remember that you still have much to discover about my creation."

"But if we'd been here earlier we could have helped Nadia," I protested. "Her whole castle looks a mess now."

Maybe I felt frustrated at being powerless. Maybe I wanted to use my own power, not the Lord God's – and that would have been a big mistake.

"Zephan," the King's Son said, "you still have not learnt about people. As you can see, Nadia and many of her new friends have forgotten me. I can make my presence known, as you have seen, but I cannot interfere where I am not wanted."

"But Nadia had so *many* new friends," I objected. "They can't *all* have forgotten you."

"No, indeed not all," the King's Son replied. "It is only a few who have caused the trouble, but they have driven the others away. They have convinced them there is no point in bothering with Nadia any more."

"Then you must *make* Nadia want to know you again," I cried in frustration.

The King's Son shook his head. "Do you *still* not understand, Zephan? I cannot *make* people do anything. They have free will to do as they please. Every hour. Every day." He smiled at us. "I did not create people to be like angels, who were given only one choice."

"And I chose to serve you at creation," I added.

"You did indeed, Zephan, and so did you, Talora. You know I love you both, but I have a very special love for people. That is why I had to die on the cross – the Lamb of God taking the punishment Nadia and everyone else deserves, to give them freedom and forgiveness."

"But everything was going so well when we last saw Nadia," I protested. "You were all enjoying the party in front of the castle."

Again the King's Son shook his head sorrowfully. "we were, indeed, and I am sad that the rejoicing should have turned to this. Self-Pleasing has been walking up and down outside Castle Nadia making new friends. Come with me now and you will see that Nadia does not recognise me. It is as though she and these friends have made themselves blind."

"Perhaps if you were to stand at the castle door they'd come to you, seeking forgiveness again," Talora suggested.

The King's Son smiled. "They know I am here, Talora, but they take no notice of me. Look up. Nadia is no longer flying the white flag. She still belongs to me, but I doubt if any other castle around would know."

"Are you going *away?*" Talora asked in alarm.

"If I walked away from here," the King's Son said, "do you think Nadia would call me back? You will see how some of her friends have become more interested in pleasing themselves than pleasing me."

That, of course, was the trouble with letting someone like Self-Pleasing join in the fun. "Will you really go?" I asked. "Surely you love Nadia too much to do that."

"I have laid out a special party for Nadia and her friends

tonight, but they have refused my invitation. Self-Pleasing has also laid out a party, and they have agreed to go there instead."

Talora and I stood on each side of the Prince and held his hands tightly. "*Please* don't give up," I begged. "Nadia needs you here."

"Then she must see that for herself. Let go of me, Zephan. Let go of me, Talora. I am going now, back across the River to my Father's throne in the Heavenly City."

Of course we stood aside, but I need hardly tell you we did it reluctantly. With tears in our eyes we watched the King's Son walk slowly away from Nadia. Not one of Nadia's friends pleaded with him to stay. Nadia didn't even notice him go.

We followed the King's Son as far as the River. When we got there he told us to rest after our escape from Shadow Hill, then to go back to Nadia who needed our help.

"And Max?" I asked.

The King's Son smiled. "You will be seeing Max very soon," he said.

I wasn't sure what the King's Son meant by that. I looked across the River. This wasn't the ordinary sort of river that runs through the countryside, where families sit down for picnics. I've already said it divides people from the land of the Heavenly City. Although angels can come and go across it, shadow angels can't. The Lord God has banned them from Heaven forever.

There is, however, a narrow path that leads to the Bridge, a wooden Cross fixed deeply into the rock of the riverbed. The arms of the Cross reach from one bank to the other, and are the way across, the Way that allows people to get in touch with the Lord God.

Before this Bridge was here – and by the way, the King's Son not only had to build it himself, he had to pay for it – it was very difficult to contact the Creator God. But now people can speak to him at any time. Indeed, he encourages everyone who belongs to him to use this Bridge all day and every day to keep in touch.

We said goodbye to the King's Son, and sat by the River to rest.

Talora saw them first – Max coming slowly to the water's edge with an old man. Max kept calling him Granddad. I must say Max's grandfather looked happy and at peace as he shielded his eyes to catch sight of the golden hills of the Heavenly City in the far distance. Max was in tears. Slowly his grandfather put one foot in the River. Then he put the next foot in and turned to wave.

Max shouted, "No!" but his grandfather just smiled and was soon waist-deep. The River was running swiftly far out, but it was calm near the bank – although very deep.

"Come back, Granddad, I don't want you to go," Max called as the old man was sinking deeper. Then as his shoulders started to get covered, Max's grandfather raised his arms, with his eyes fixed on the hills in the far distance.

"Look," Talora said, pointing. "See, some angels are coming."

Suddenly the angels picked Max's grandfather safely out of the water before it could cover him. As he was lifted into the air he turned and called to Max. "We'll meet again one day, Max. May God bless you and keep you."

Then he was gone, carried to safety.

Talora looked at me, excitement in her eyes. "The Lord God said I could help take Nadia to the Heavenly City one day. Oh, Zephan, maybe we'll be allowed to take Max and other people there as well."

"If they belong to the Lord God."

"Then we must *make* them," Talora insisted.

I shook my head. "Remember – the Lord God lets everyone choose."

"But we chose, too, Zephan. Chose to serve the Lord God when we were created."

"We had one choice, Talora, and one choice only. If at creation we chose to disobey, there was no forgiveness, no way back. The Lord God loves his people in a very different way, and always forgives them when they ask to be forgiven."

A little later two people appeared with another elderly man. This time there were no smiles, only tears. I recognised the two who had come with him – Good-Deeds and Great-Hopes. When I say I recognised them, I mean that they looked very much like the creatures with the same names that had been making such a nuisance of themselves at Castle Nadia. But these creatures must belong to the old man.

The old man clung tightly to Good-Deeds. "Stay with me," he begged. "I need you now, more than I've ever needed anything."

Good-Deeds and Great-Hopes pulled themselves away. "We cannot go with you," Good-Deeds told him. "We count for nothing on the other side. You have to go alone."

"But I had such great hopes that all would be well," the old man said. "I've done so many good deeds in my life. Please come with me."

He put one foot in the River and tried to withdraw it quickly. The chill of the water must have scared him, but it seemed he had no choice but to continue wading in deeper and deeper to where the water ran fastest.

No angels came to carry him to safety as he disappeared from sight.

CHAPTER 30

Flames

That evening Nadia and many of her friends crowded round to the back of the castle where Self-Pleasing had laid out his great treat. They had obviously forgotten that the King's Son had invited them to a party of his own. We could sense excitement in the air as we slipped unnoticed amongst the group. Not one of them seemed aware that a line of wooden shacks had reappeared recently against the walls of Castle Nadia, built of old, rotting wood. I suppose it sometimes helps to have these things pointed out, but I knew no one would listen if I said anything. I thought I recognised two of Max's friends here, which surprised me.

"I trust you've all come to enjoy yourselves," Self-Pleasing shouted from the top table. "You are Nadia's true friends, and you have every right to be here."

Nadia and her friends sat down and started to eat. The host looked delighted as he glanced around the tables. Everyone seemed to be having such fun. Suddenly Self-Pleasing jumped up and strode angrily to where a girl was sitting alone. She had no food with her.

"Are you feeling unwell?" Self-Pleasing asked loudly.

Everyone stopped eating to look at the girl.

"What is your name, and why don't you eat?" Self-Pleasing

shouted, when the girl made no reply. "You must speak to me if you don't want to be thrown out of this wonderful party."

"My name is Love-God," the girl said quietly.

"*Love-God?* What sort of name is *Love-God*?" Self-Pleasing demanded.

"That is my name," the girl replied. "You may ask the others if you wish."

"It is," someone called. "It's a silly name, but that's what she's called."

Everyone laughed.

"Well, it's a very strange name if you ask me." Self-Pleasing's frown turned to a smile. "Come now, Love-God, don't sit there all alone. Join in the festivities. Eat and drink, and you will soon be as merry as the rest of us."

Love-God shook her head. "I am a friend of Nadia," she said. "I came here to enjoy the party, but now ..." Then she began to cry. Love-God, surely, belonged to the Lord God in the way that Self-Pleasing and his companions belonged to Diabolus.

Nadia and her friends didn't seem so merry now, looking guilty for the way they'd been living.

"Cheer up," Self-Pleasing said to Love-God with a big smile. "We don't want any unhappiness here. Perhaps you're tired and need a good sleep."

Love-God wiped her eyes. "You're right, I am sad, but it's not because of the food or because I'm tired. Nadia has grieved the King's Son. The white flag is no longer flying. I do not believe he is in Castle Nadia any more."

"What nonsense!" Self-Pleasing told her irritably. "Why, even from here we can see Nadia's white flag on top of her castle." He paused. "True, it's ... it's not flying very high today, but I'm sure you'd be able to see it if you were standing up high enough." He clapped his hands. "Come on, this is no time for anyone to be sad."

Conscience stood up. "Love-God is right. Nadia's flag is no longer flying." He turned to Nadia's friends. "And where are your banners that you carried so boldly all those months ago?"

Everyone hung their heads in shame as they admitted that they'd not bothered to talk with the Prince for many weeks. Some said they'd not talked with him for even longer than that. Nadia looked more ashamed than the others, and she ran into her castle crying.

"You're nothing but a nuisance," Self-Pleasing said to Love-God. "What right have you to upset Nadia and her friends at a time of great happiness such as this? Shame on you. Now leave us alone!"

Love-God stood up slowly and walked away into the valley.

I could stay silent no longer. I jumped on the nearest table and said I'd seen the King's Son leaving the castle, unnoticed. Of course, saying something like that was asking for trouble, for Self-Pleasing immediately recognised me as his prisoner from the cave and he tried to grab hold of me. But as he reached out, Nadia ran from her castle gripping something tightly in her hands, holding it out in front like a sword.

And indeed it was a weapon – it was the Holy Book the King's Son had given Nadia earlier. From the look of it, it hadn't seen much use. The cover seemed like new, and the pages inside unworn. Even so, it made a very sharp weapon.

"You've led us astray," she told Self-Pleasing as she opened the Book. "We listened to you, and believed you had much to offer. But it says here you're an enemy of the Lord God. His Son told us to destroy *all* his enemies."

With this speech everyone turned on Self-Pleasing, but he escaped into one of the wooden shacks behind the castle, slamming the door shut. We could hear him pushing several bolts into place as the angry crowd gathered outside.

"Burn the place down!" Conscience shouted.

"Yes, burn the place down, and burn Self-Pleasing with it!" Nadia called out.

Talora stood with me while Nadia set fire to the rotten wood. As the flames leapt high into the night sky, I saw a sudden movement among the bushes and thought I caught a glimpse of Self-Pleasing running away. What that possible?

Now, that might have been the end of things, a happy end, but I sensed something evil nearby. A few flaps of our wings took us high into the air, before we swooped across the open countryside to Shadow Hill. There we found Diabolus watching from the wood. We saw him shudder as the flames from Self-Pleasing's house lit the night sky, squirming uncomfortably as though he felt himself to be on fire.

"That castle will be mine one day," we heard him mutter angrily. "The King's Son will never be able to hold such a place against my mighty army!"

We certainly didn't wait around, but flew quickly back to Castle Nadia. In the way that we can sense evil, shadow angels can sense goodness and love – and they don't like sensing us any more than we like sensing them.

When we got back, the fire had burnt itself out and Self-Pleasing's shack was just a pile of glowing embers. Nadia and her friends stayed watching, excited that they'd found the courage to destroy Self-Pleasing's house. But I was pretty certain that its owner had escaped into the night.

CHAPTER 31

Messages

The next morning a heavy darkness hung over Castle Nadia. Love-God stood outside the castle door and told everyone that they'd been foolish to forget about meeting with the King's Son every day, or to come to his feasts.

Nadia listened carefully. "I am undefended," she said in alarm. "I forgot to check who was building around my castle. I've not cared for my armour, and last night was the first time I used my Sword for ages. What am I to do?"

Some of Nadia's friends said the same thing as they walked around in confusion. Knowledge appeared and stood in front of them. I remembered how the King's Son had appointed him earlier as the Keeper of Wisdom to help Nadia, but no one seemed to know who he was. Perhaps they'd not seen him around for some time. I wondered if he'd still make a reliable leader.

"Listen, everyone," Knowledge said. "There is only one thing to do. You must each send a message to the King's Son."

"What do I write?" Nadia asked.

A general murmur went up from Nadia's friends, for they clearly wanted Knowledge to tell them exactly what to put in their letters.

"Do you want to know the King's Son again?" Knowledge

asked.

Everyone did.

"Then I'm sure you can think of the right thing to say. I will deliver the messages myself." With that, he walked away.

And that was it.

Nadia and her friends discussed among themselves what they should each write. One friend said he ought to admit he'd forgotten the Lord God, while another thought it would be a good idea to admit that her memories of the King's Son had grown faint. Another said she was going to ask the Lord to have mercy, and ask him to keep her safe.

Some of the messages were long, but I could see that many were just a few lines. What did they say? It's not for me to read other people's letters, but I guessed everyone was pleading for forgiveness so that they could know the King's Son again.

"I will use the Bridge over the River to take your messages to the court of the Lord God of Heaven," Knowledge announced, as he climbed on his horse. "I believe I shall find his Son there."

Then he galloped off, clutching the letters tightly with one hand and the reins with the other. Nadia and her friends said every word of their letters had been carefully written, so they hoped the King's Son would make himself known to them again – as soon as he'd read them.

A little later we heard a buzz of excitement. Knowledge was back in a cloud of dust, his face far from happy. "The door of Heaven was shut," he explained gloomily.

"Did you knock?" Nadia asked.

"I knocked," Knowledge said.

"Did you knock hard?" one of Nadia's friends called out.

"I knocked hard, and I knocked for a long time. A guard came out and asked me why I'd come. I explained why I was there, and the guard told me to keep hold of your letters and wait. I waited a long time but no one came to the door. And now I've come back."

"Go and try again," Choosing pleaded. "And wait longer this time."

Knowledge sighed, but agreed to return once more to Heaven with the messages. It wasn't long before he was back to say that again he'd been told to wait for an answer. He'd not waited, because it seemed to him that no answer would come.

"So here I am," he explained sadly.

Nadia began to cry, and this set everyone off. "Let's all go and meet with the King's Son, and beg him to return," she said.

That night, the Bridge across the River was full of messengers coming and going. Talora and I could see that they each carried their own letters, pleading with the King for his Son to speak to them again but, like Knowledge, no one was prepared to wait for an answer. The next night the same thing happened. And the next night.

As you can imagine, with all this coming and going there was quite a lot of noise. Talora said we ought to pay another visit to the Shadowed Wood and see if the companions of Diabolus had noticed what was going on.

CHAPTER 32

Self-Pleasing Again

As we pushed our way through the horrible trees, we could still sense evil in the air. And there, sheltering in the cave, we found the creatures that had tied us up earlier – including Self-Pleasing. I'd suspected at the time that Self-Pleasing had escaped from the burning shack, but I couldn't think how he'd done it. The creatures were busy writing a letter of their own by the flickering light of their fire. From their chatter we realised that they were planning revenge on Nadia and her friends for trying to contact the King's Son.

So, even while Nadia and her friends were sending their letters to the King, this evil lot sent a letter of their own to their leader. Now, that's the sort of letter that needs to be read. Invisible to these creatures – although they occasionally shifted uneasily – I leant over their shoulders and read:

> *To our Great Lord Diabolus,*
> *We beg you to remove the disgrace that the King's Son has done to Castle Nadia and other castles in this place. Nadia and her new friends will be at your mercy, for they have been unable to contact the King's Son. If you capture Castle Nadia you can be sure we will come to your help immediately.*

It sounded a scary letter, but first it had to be delivered. Maybe with Talora's help I could snatch it from them. Self-Pleasing, the leader of the gang, agreed to act as messenger. I still don't know how it happened, but Self-Pleasing managed to get out of the cave with the letter before I could do anything. Talora put her foot out to trip him up, but he staggered away into the darkness and disappeared. The evil companions in the group looked puzzled to see Self-Pleasing stumble, so at least it gave them something to worry about!

While the gang was waiting for Self-Pleasing to return, I took the opportunity to glance round the cave. The only thing that looked new was a pile of large bags at the back. They seemed to be full but I had no idea what was in them, and if I started to open them the creatures would be sure to notice.

It seemed a long wait before Self-Pleasing came back, but he looked excited as he pulled a grubby letter from his pocket just as the sun was rising through the unhealthy trees. He read it aloud to everyone's great delight – well, to everyone's great delight except mine and Talora's.

> *My Dear Self-Pleasing,*
>
> *How excited I am to learn that Nadia and her new friends are no longer talking to the King's Son. How happy I am to hear that you are all well, for I want you to put my plan into action to destroy Castle Nadia and the castles of Nadia's new friends. I have already instructed you what to do, and I know you have prepared well. So set out as soon as it is dark. Tonight.*
>
> *Your Caring Master,*
> *Diabolus*

"Will you take *me* with you?" a voice growled from the heavy shadows.

"*You*?" Self-Pleasing said in disgust. "Why would I take *you*?"

"My name is Self-Righteous," his companion said, emerging into the firelight. "I can do a lot of damage."

"Indeed, yes." Self-Pleasing sounded thoughtful. "You could certainly help smash Castle Nadia to the ground, and then ..." He paused and licked his lips.

"Yes?" his companions asked together.

"Then we will rebuild it especially for Nadia, using the plans Diabolus will give us."

The creatures let out a scream of triumph.

"Please let me go with you," another said, emerging into the light.

"Certainly, Forgetfulness." Self-Pleasing scratched his chin. "Diabolus said you are like a poison. Poisoning Nadia would seem like a good idea."

Everyone smiled, although some looked disappointed at the thought that Self-Pleasing might not choose them.

"What about me?" a voice asked from the shadows.

"Ah yes, Profane. Diabolus mentioned you and your foul mouth. Vile, he said. He thought someone like you could undermine the walls." Self-Pleasing grinned and turned to a creature that had been silent until now. He pointed at him. "Won't-Believe," he said, "step forward. Diabolus says you are a helper whom he trusts greatly."

Won't-Believe bowed. "You *must* take me."

Self-Pleasing roared with laughter. "I have decided to take *all* of you!"

"Do we have to disguise ourselves, as ..." Won't-Believe hesitated. "As you did?"

The gasp of horror must have been heard as far away as Castle Nadia.

"You were nearly burnt alive," a shrill chorus went up, but Self-Pleasing shouted so loudly that everyone stopped.

"Enough of that!" he snapped angrily. "I had the foresight to build an escape tunnel that came out in the bushes. You must all learn a lesson from me, and plan ahead."

"Will we be doing battle against the King's Son?" Forgetfulness asked. "I'm not a fighter, I just poison people's minds so that they forget the K… Forget … *him*." He clutched his stomach and pulled a face. "I remember what happened to our friends Hate, Anger, Greed and Dishonesty. The King's followers have a Sword that is sharper than anything we possess."

The others clutched their stomachs too. "A very sharp Sword," they agreed.

"Now that I think about it, perhaps we need not *all* go," Forgetfulness suggested. "Suppose some of you were to go on ahead. You could offer to become great friends with Nadia, and I might not be needed."

"I've just told you, we're *all* going," Self-Pleasing yelled. Then he lowered his voice. "Some of you have already been given important tasks. So now I'm just waiting for Great-Hopes."

Talora nudged me. "Zephan," she whispered, almost in panic, "I thought Great-Hopes from Castle Nadia was dead."

"The King's Son stripped him of his armour, but he ran away," I reminded her. "He must have recovered."

"Then there's going to be trouble."

I nodded. "There's going to be trouble all right. Big trouble."

CHAPTER 33

Max

"Great-Hopes should be here by now." Self-Pleasing sounded angry as the afternoon wore on. "I'm going out to find him. The rest of you wait here."

Of course I wanted to rush forward with Talora and shout for the King's Son to come and destroy these creatures. But if we could interfere like that – and believe me, we often want to – people would be like robots with no free choice. It may be hard to understand, but it's true.

"Do you remember Max?" The voice from behind made us jump. Well, we recognised who it was immediately. The King's Son seemed to be able to talk to us without these companions of Diabolus hearing.

"We've not seen him for some time," I said. "But we often think about him."

"I want you to go to him now," the King's Son told us.

"Now?" I couldn't help thinking that this seemed a strange time to leave the cave, just as something big was about to happen. Nadia was the one in danger. Or ... or maybe Max was in danger too. The Lord God had told us to help care for both of them.

"Go and see him right away," the King's Son said.

It was unlikely this evil gang would leave just yet. Diabolus had ordered them to attack Castle Nadia tonight when it was dark, and that was a few hours away. Anyway, if the King's Son says I have to go, then I have to go. It's not for angels to question his plans.

"Talora, you are to go with Zephan," the King's Son added. "Max will need you both."

And so we went. We found Max on his own, round the back of his castle, wearing tough gloves. He was dealing with a patch of brambles that were already threatening to reach his windows. Someone had started to build a wooden shack against the back wall. Maybe Max hadn't seen it – it would surely be the first thing he'd knock down if he knew it was there. We'd been watching some of the creatures that built these shacks outside Castle Nadia, and lived in them, and knew what a nuisance they could be.

Max looked up at us and smiled. "Welcome," he said.

I have to say we were surprised, because we thought we were invisible. Maybe the Lord God wanted it this way. Anyhow, Max seemed at ease. Almost certainly he couldn't see our wings.

"You look busy," I said. I know it wasn't anything profound, but it's the sort of thing angels tend to say to open a conversation

"Just doing a spot of gardening," Max explained cheerfully. He didn't stop working while he spoke, but kept glancing up at us as he continued hacking away at the sharp thorns. "You wouldn't believe how often I have to do this." He pulled his hand back quickly as a sharp thorn pierced his glove. "Every day there's something to sort out around my castle."

"Whose building is that?" Talora asked.

Max looked puzzled. "Building?"

"This one," I said, banging on the wood.

"Oh, *that* building. I've not really thought about it before. I've been too busy clearing these brambles."

"We could help you knock it down," I offered.

Max shrugged. "Is it a problem?"

"It's going to be a problem soon," I told him.

Talora agreed with me. "Just get rid of it now," she said.

Max dropped his sharp knife and examined the shack. "Do you think anyone is inside?"

I must admit I was too nervous to risk poking my head through the door. "Get some matches," I said. "The wood looks rotten." I remembered how Self-Pleasing's house had burnt easily at Castle Nadia, and hopefully the occupant of this one didn't have an escape tunnel.

Max ran indoors and returned with matches and a sharp Sword. *The Sword of God* was engraved along the blade in gleaming letters that seemed to burn our eyes. This must be what was written on Nadia's Sword.

Max twisted the Sword in his firm grasp and I could see that the letters on the other side were slightly different. The letter *S* was missing. The words, glittering and flaring, now read *The Word of God*. I smiled to myself. Yes, the Word of God *is* the Sword of God. Max obviously understood it, and was prepared to put his Sword to good use.

"You're right," Max told me. "Nasty things live in these places. Sometimes they keep whispering to me all day long. It gets better when I talk to the King's Son and ask for his help. Even so, I fail him – ever so often."

"What do you do then?" Talora asked.

Max smiled. "I ask him for forgiveness. Do you know Nadia? She's in the castle over there."

I said we did.

"I thought I'd seen the two of you there." Max waved his

Sword in the air and took a practice lunge. "Nadia didn't bother to keep asking for forgiveness, and then she forgot all about the King's Son. That's why it's all gone wrong for her and for some of her friends. Even for two of my friends."

I pointed to the wooden building. "Are you going to use your Sword on that?"

Max's eyes gleamed. "I'm going to smash it down. Then we can burn it." He thrust his Sword at the wooden boards but it bounced back and nearly cut his leg.

Max tutted to himself. "Whoops, I shouldn't have tried that alone. Lord God," he said quietly, "please help me."

I could see now why the King's Son had sent us here.

"Lord God," Max repeated. "Please help me." As he spoke, Max looked at me and our eyes locked. I just nodded.

"*You?*" he said grinning. "You're the help I've just asked for? You came to help me before I even *asked*? What a great God we have." Then he closed his eyes for a moment and whispered a prayer of thanks to the King's Son.

"We'll deal with it together," I said.

The handle of the Sword was large enough for the three of us to hold. We pulled the Sword back and thrust it powerfully through the side of the low building. Something inside screamed, but Max didn't seem concerned.

"Now I'll set light to the place," he said calmly.

The flames leapt up as soon as Max put a match to it. No further screams came from inside. The Sword must have finished off whatever had been in there.

"Look at those clouds," Max said suddenly, pointing to the sky as the shack collapsed into ashes. "It's going to rain soon. A big storm. I'd better go inside, but I'll be out again tomorrow. There's always something to do. And thanks ever so much for your help."

"No," I said firmly, "don't thank us. You must thank the Lord God. That's the way it works."

I waved my hand and smiled. Not so much a farewell as a see-you-again-soon.

"I'll thank him now," Max called. "Come again. I've enjoyed meeting you."

With that he went inside, shutting the castle door and bolting it firmly. He didn't ask who we were or where we'd come from. Perhaps he was too busy with his gardening to think about it.

Or perhaps he guessed.

"Come on," I said to Talora, realising Max was right – the weather did look extremely threatening. "We'd better fly back to the cave on Shadow Hill."

CHAPTER 34

The Showmen

The cave was empty when we reached it, with not even a glow from the fire to break the gloom, and the ashes felt barely warm. Had we left it too late? No, the King's Son must have a plan for Nadia. Surely he would never have sent us to Castle Max if it left Nadia in greater danger.

It was dusk when we flew towards the hill where Castle Nadia stood, walking the last part of the way so as not to attract attention. The storm clouds had certainly been building up for the past couple of hours, but it wasn't raining yet. To our surprise we found visitors busily unpacking their wares. Nadia and her friends stood in a group, examining brightly coloured and mysterious objects.

Within what seemed minutes – I'm not very good at judging time – the strangers had put up a set of fairground tents, lit by the flames of burning torches fixed up high on posts. A clown ran from the first tent, laughing and joking. He scooped a small furry creature from one of his huge pockets and held it up, wriggling.

"It's a gisko!" Talora gasped. "How did he get one of those, Zephan? Did you bring it with you from Eltor?

"It's not a gisko," I told her. "The hair is too smooth."

"This is a gopher," the clown shouted. "And now I'm going to eat it!"

To gasps from Nadia and her friends, he tipped his head back and opened his mouth wide. It was obviously a conjuring trick, but a very good one. Everyone seemed convinced the clown had swallowed the animal whole.

He pulled another gopher from his pocket to great applause, and proceeded to "swallow" it too, although it was probably the same animal as before. For a clown he didn't seem particularly well dressed. His costume was worn and badly patched in places, but his act seemed to be going down well – just like his gophers.

"Who are you?" someone called.

"I eat gophers for fun," the clown shouted. "And that is my name."

As if by magic he unrolled a large banner with the name *Eat Gophers – the Incredible Clown*. Nadia's friends laughed even more at that, and applauded loudly again. I noticed Nadia making her way to the front, and apparently so did the clown. He smiled at her and called her forward.

But before Nadia could get there, a showman emerged from the adjoining tent, flinging the canvas door wide open. Inside I could see a shooting gallery with a range of targets, and what looked like very expensive prizes.

"Come and hit the target," the showman called. "Don't worry about it being hard work. These guns almost shoot themselves. You can forget all your cares and worries with one of these. See the sign above the targets, and believe it."

The sign said *Effortless Gun*, and the people certainly did believe it. They pushed forward to try their luck.

In the third tent we saw someone dressed in a white surgeon's coat hang a notice on the outside of the tent flap. *Open Far* it said. *Painless Dentist*. I admit I was puzzled. A fourth tent flap opened and someone dressed in the old-fashioned black gown and mortarboard of a schoolmaster emerged to announce a spelling competition.

"Come and test your spelling, just for fun," he called. "Come in. Just spell some simple words. A prize every time. You'll be safe. There's no punishment for mistakes. That's why this is my name." With that he produced a large chalkboard from inside the tent and stood it on the grass. *Safe Spelling* it said.

The showman at the next tent whisked the cover off a large circular stand. You may have seen a fairground stall where plastic fish or ducks swim round, with a ring on their backs. This was something similar, but instead of fish, huge black and brown slugs slid across a shiny mat. They looked real, but the rings made me think they couldn't be.

Talora shuddered when she saw them, and said she was glad we don't have things like slugs on Eltor. I explained that the air there is much too dry for creatures like that, and Talora said it was just as well. I was going to tell her you need morning dew for slugs, but this wasn't the right time to tease her about the meaning of her name.

"Catch a slug and get a prize," the showman shouted. "Every slug wins a prize. Roll up, roll up, it's free! All you have to do is hoist a slug with this rod and line. Don't forget now, it's free."

He unrolled a sign from the awning that blared *Hoist Free Slug* in garish red and blue lettering. These people were up to no good, I could see that, but exactly what were they up to? I felt sure the plan of Diabolus to recapture Castle Nadia was well in hand.

A tubby showman, wearing a short brown coat, pulled back

the front flap of the last tent. "Come and taste my free sweets," he called. "Just one bite and you'll love them."

I have to admit the confections looked delicious. Angels don't normally eat sweets, but I certainly fancied some of these – especially the ones with red and green frosted stripes.

"You'll *love* them," the showman continued as Nadia's friends gathered, licking their lips. "They're *new*, so just take a *bite – one bite*!"

That was when I noticed the sign above his stall that read *Love New Bite*. Everyone pushed forward for their free sample.

I looked for Nadia, but she had wandered off. I wanted to search for her, but Talora suggested we stay and see what these showmen really wanted. If only we could see their faces more clearly we might recognise them, but the burning torches were fixed up too high, casting their faces into shadow.

At last we saw Nadia emerge from the tent of the dentist *Open Far* and run to her friends, using the name of the King's Son as a swear word. Her friends laughed and said they must get their mouths seen to. They came out one by one, using words that they would have been ashamed to use before the showmen pitched their tents here.

Those who had taken the *Safe Spelling* test also seemed pleased with themselves. They told their friends that if they could all enjoy themselves like this, life would be great.

"Something bad is happening," Talora whispered.

Too right it was. The clown with the name *Eat Gophers* was willing to share some of his tricks with everyone, promising to show them how to perform amazing magic.

"I can show you magic that is so good you need have no fear for the future, because you will be able to control what happens to you. Things will work out well – and that's a promise!"

I moved to the shooting gallery. The stall seemed to live up to its name of *Effortless Gun,* for people fired the weapons time after time without becoming tired, always winning marvellous prizes. I think they'd have gone on shooting all evening if they could, forgetting where they were and what time it was.

Other friends of Nadia were busy catching plastic slugs on the *Hoist Free Slugs* stall. I must say they looked extremely pleased with themselves, as though they had genuine talent. But all they had to do was catch hold of a ring, using a rod and line with a hook on the end – hardly a skilful task. Still they couldn't help boasting about how well they'd done, whispering among themselves that they were the most clever people at the fair.

The most popular stall was *Love New Bite* where everyone was indulging in the free sweets – and obviously finding them irresistible. All they wanted to do was enjoy themselves, having seemed to have forgotten they belonged to the Lord God and his family.

I was struggling to understand what was going on, but Talora figured it out first.

"Look carefully at the signs," she whispered.

"Are there clues somewhere?" I asked. "Why, what have you discovered?"

"What happens when people win prizes on the *Hoist Free Slug* stall?"

Talora seemed in a teasing mood, but I think all she wanted was to make me think the answers through properly. I mean, it was all right to be teasing each other on Eltor, but this was dangerous territory.

"They look as though they're marvellous and can do noth-ing wrong. So?"

"And what happens when they learn to do tricks from the clown *Eat Gophers*?"

"They seem to think they can carry out some sort of magic, and everything will be all right."

"Zephan, doesn't that give you a clue? What happens when someone visits the dentist, *Open Far*?

"They all seem to come out swearing," I said. "And I don't like hearing it. Not from people who claim to belong to the King's Son."

"Tell me the dentist's name again."

"*Open Far*," I repeated.

"Read it again, but mix the letters up."

Angels are astute readers, especially when it comes to reading scrolls. Some even write on walls. Well, I personally know an angel who is an expert on graffiti, and once wrote *Mene, Mene, Tekel, Uparsin* in huge letters on the wall of a palace in Babylon – but I'm sure he'd want me to make it clear to you that the Lord God asked him to do it. If you want to know what those words mean, you'll have to read about Belshazzar in the book of Daniel in your own Sword – your Bible.

I know we angels are supposed to be bright, and quick learners, but it took me a time to catch on to what Talora had already discovered. It was only when I wrote down *Open Far* and moved the letters around that I got it. "He's *Profane*! We saw him in the cave!"

"And *Eat Gophers* the clown?"

I shuffled those letters around. "That's *Great Hopes*! This is terrible. *Hoist Free Slug* is ..."

"*Self-Righteous*," Talora finished. "The man pretending to be a teacher running the *Safe Spelling* competition is *Self-Pleasing*. No wonder everyone comes out thinking they can be free to please themselves in life."

I wanted to guess the last two names. It seemed easy now.

Effortless Gun, the showman with the shooting gallery, was *Forgetfulness. Love New Bite* was their plump companion, *Won't-Believe*. Yes, now it all made sense. These tents and stalls must have been packed inside the sacks we saw inside the cave on Shadow Hill.

Suddenly Nadia stood up and clapped her hands. "Well," she called as everyone turned to listen, "I think we're all doing pretty well. If the King's Son comes this way again – and perhaps he never will – I know he'll be pleased with the things we can do. He certainly won't blame us for anything."

Sadly, everyone agreed. The companions of Diabolus were here, and we had to do something quickly to spoil their plans.

Talora looked at me in alarm. "Why have Nadia and her friends given up sending messages to the Lord God? Tell me, Zephan. Can't they understand he still loves them?"

"This castle's in a sad state," I said. "Let's see if we can talk some sense into Nadia and her friends."

The only way to join them was to make ourselves visible. Making ourselves visible and invisible is something only angels can do, so there's no point in me telling you how it's done. Not that becoming visible did much good, for no matter how hard we pleaded with them to call out to the Lord God for help, Nadia and her friends took no notice. However, they knew something was different about us, even though I'm sure they couldn't see our wings.

As we walked about wearing the bright and dazzling white of Heaven, everyone laughed and pointed at us. We had to expose the showmen for the frauds and deceivers they were.

That was when the rain came.

CHAPTER 35

A Fresh Attack

The massive storm clouds, which had been racing in from the west since we left Castle Max, finally arrived in their fullest force. Because it never rains on Eltor, I hadn't seen such wet weather for thousands of years, and Talora looked so startled that I decided she'd never, ever seen rain before – certainly not torrential rain like this. The clouds lit up inside with fierce lightning while the rain lashed everything in sight.

We clung together tightly as thunder crashed all around us. Angels are waterproof in normal circumstances, but these heavy windswept raindrops stung our faces. I raised my wings and folded them over my head like an umbrella, but the rain came through regardless.

Nadia and her friends screamed and ran back to their castles to avoid getting soaked by the deluge. Nadia slammed her door shut and we could hear her bolting it. The showmen's tents were awash, and as the stakes holding them securely upright gave way, they began to slide down the hill. First slowly, then faster and faster until they were swept out of sight. Well, some good was coming of this storm. I wondered if the Lord God had sent it for this very reason.

Talora found us an overhanging rock we could use for shelter. We would have flown a distance beyond the storm, but the rain had soaked our wings, making flight decidedly dangerous in a windy situation like this. So we settled down in our makeshift refuge and waited for morning. I kept wondering if the slugs and sweets and other things were gone for good – along with the showmen.

The rain must have stopped overnight, but we didn't notice. We were soaked and exhausted, and slept until the sun was already climbing high in a blue sky. The dark clouds were just distant shapes on the horizon, and the birds had returned to their lively twittering. Our wings had dried out during the night, and we felt warm and rested.

The first thing we saw was that the creatures were still alive, and had been busy during the night rebuilding their shacks round the back of Castle Nadia. It was what you on Earth call springtime, and the sun felt warm and life-giving.

The door of one of the shacks was partly open, and we could hear whispering inside. "Very soon now the army of Diabolus will be here. Every day he watches to see . . ."

Talora pulled me back as a shadow angel darted out of the door and looked around sharply.

"Lord God, make us invisible to his eyes," Talora whispered.

The shadow angel muttered something angrily to himself before going back inside, pulling the door tightly shut. He sensed, for sure, that we were around.

"What can we do?" I asked urgently. "These shacks are going to be securely finished soon. If only Nadia would raise her flag and show everyone she still belongs to the King's Son. I'm sure it would help."

"Nadia and her friends must send another message to the King," Talora said firmly. "They simply *must!*"

"But they've already done that. We saw them. They've sent

lots of messages."

"True," Talora agreed. "But if they were deep down sorry, surely they would have waited longer to get an answer."

I sat with Talora for the rest of the day, hoping Nadia or her friends would reappear. Angels don't wear watches, but when darkness fell I knew we were unlikely to see anyone from the nearby castles until the next morning.

"Please, can I talk to you?"

The voice from behind made us jump with fright. A girl stood there in the darkness. The only way we could see her was by the light from her shimmering robe

"You're Love-God," I said, remembering how she had spoilt the party for Self-Pleasing.

Love-God smiled, and obviously recognised us from that time as well. "You must have seen how the companions of Diabolus are building again at the back of Castle Nadia," she said, with a worried look on her face. "I have to find Nadia and her friends and warn them."

"Do they still have the Swords that the King's Son gave them?" Talora asked.

Love-God sighed. "They do, but the blades have grown ever so dull and rusty. I'm going to tell them that they can still use their Swords to seek out and destroy all that's wrong in their lives. While I'm doing that, I'd like you check what's happening on Shadow Hill."

Even though it was dark, I agreed to take Talora with me and see what we could find. Did Love-God know we were angels? Possibly not, although with that shimmering robe she clearly wasn't an ordinary person either.

We waited until Love-God was out of sight, and then flew high above Castle Nadia before drifting silently towards Shadow Hill. When I say silently, I mean we let our wings rise and fall gently, using the air currents to maintain a good height without needing to flap too enthusiastically.

The moon gave just enough light to guide us as we approached the Shadowed Wood. Talora caught hold of my foot. "Down there," she whispered. "I saw a brief flicker of a flame. Just for a moment."

As our eyes took in the gloomy landscape, we started to see occasional flares of light on the ground. People seemed to be moving around, concealing their flaming torches from anyone above. I knew immediately what was down there – an army using their shields to hide from the Lord God's angels!

There was only one thing to do, and that meant risking being seen and captured. With our wings spread out high above our heads we dropped as silently as we could to the ground close to the camp. Then we did what good spies should do: we made our way towards the enemy, to watch and listen – while trying not to be caught again.

CHAPTER 36

The Army of Doubters

"They're very close," I reported to Love-God early the next morning. "They're an army calling themselves the Doubters. I reckon there could be as many as two hundred of them. Do you remember someone called Won't-Believe? We've discovered that he has someone called All-Except-Me helping him, and they could all be here within the hour."

Love-God said she had found Nadia, who didn't want to be told about any danger. So Love-God called a meeting with her special friends. I was glad to see she now considered Choosing a friend, which indicated to me that he was seeing sense at last.

"The Doubters are coming," Love-God told them. "All-Except-Me is with them, and we all know what that means."

"What do you think we should do?" Choosing asked, sounding surprisingly calm.

"I suggest Nadia sends another message to the Lord God, pleading for help," Love-God said.

Choosing shook his head. "He didn't reply to her pleas last time. Nadia is afraid she's hurt him too much. She doubts he will come again with love and forgiveness."

Love-God clapped her hands. "Choosing, you are *wrong*. We must encourage Nadia to *keep* asking. The last thing she needs now is to be caught by the army of doubters."

A cry went up from the valley below the castle. Nadia's special friends – the friends who had also decided to come to the King's Son earlier but had since rejected him – had been making their way to see her. Now they ran towards us in panic, shouting that they'd seen soldiers approaching from Shadow Hill.

When she heard the noise, Nadia hurried to the top of her castle and looked down in alarm from the battlements surrounding the flat roof. Choosing ordered her to come back down and let him enter Castle Nadia with Love-God. Once safely inside, we could hear them helping Nadia set the iron bars and bolts firmly in place. Then they began to run up the stairs.

"You must go to the Holy Spirit in his secret room," Choosing told Nadia, sounding out of breath. I don't think he liked being rushed into making a decision. Or maybe it was the long flight of steps that made him sound exhausted. "Ask the Holy Spirit to help you write a new message to the King."

I know all this because I'd flown to one of the open windows with Talora. We weren't being nosy – but the King's Son had told us to keep an eye on Nadia. If Choosing had a fault it would be that he changed his mind too often – but better Choosing than Unchanging, and this was certainly one of his better decisions.

Nadia knocked hard on the door of the secret room where the Holy Spirit had come to live. "I need help," she called, and burst into tears.

"You have hurt and grieved the King's Son," the reply came as the door opened.

"I know," Nadia sobbed, going in slowly and kneeling down. "Please tell me what I have to do."

"You have the Word of the Lord God in writing," the Holy

Spirit told her. "Search it, and you will find the Way."

And that was all. This answer was obviously not what Nadia expected. Indeed, Choosing also began to cry, and the two sat in despair outside the room.

I noticed that Love-God was smiling. "It seems to me," she told Nadia, "that the answer contains more help than you think. The King's Son calls himself the Way in his Holy Book, so it will be through him that you must be rescued."

Nadia stopped crying, but still seemed puzzled.

"Love-God is right," Choosing said, wiping his eyes. "Ask the Lord God for forgiveness once more. And this time you must wait for the answer. The Creator God has seen your tears. Tell him that you understand his Son is the Way – the only Way to get forgiveness."

Before Nadia could do anything, her friends shouted up with news that the troops of Diabolus were retreating back towards the Shadowed Wood. When Nadia told them she was writing another letter they laughed, and said this wasn't the right time for sending messages. The army of Doubters had been driven off with no one being wounded – what more could anyone want?

"Let's go and finish them off tonight," everyone shouted. "We can earn our forgiveness by winning the battle."

The prospect of overcoming the Doubters excited Nadia so much that she told Love-God and Choosing that she'd write her letter when she got back.

As darkness fell, Nadia and her friends were still jumping up and down in anticipation.

"Come on, it's time to go and destroy Diabolus and his army of Doubters!" Nadia's friends called from the foot of her castle, where they had gathered for their anticipated easy victory.

"Destroy Diabolus and his army of Doubters!" a cry went up from all around.

"Yes," Nadia called, "we'll go and finish them off now!"

I saw Talora shiver in fright. "They mustn't go," she gasped. "How can they fight that evil army in the dark all by themselves? Shadow Hill belongs to Diabolus."

I shook my head in despair. No one was wearing the armour the King's Son had given them – all they had were their rusty Swords that they hardly ever used. Diabolus was drawing Nadia and her friends into a deadly trap.

CHAPTER 37

The Ambush

Excited, expectant voices filled the night. Unfortunately, we had no way of stopping Nadia and her friends from launching their doomed assault on the army of Doubters. I held Talora by the arm as we saw Won't-Believe and All-Except-Me emerging from the Shadowed Wood on horseback with a group of shadow angels, making their way towards Castle Nadia.

Seeing them coming stealthily, like foxes, Nadia ordered Choosing to bring three creatures called Addiction, Self and Immorality from their shacks round the back of her castle. Then, in full view of Won't-Believe, she plunged her Sword through each of them in turn.

"Are you watching?" Nadia called into the darkness. "So will perish *all* your evil companions!"

Won't-Believe watched for a moment, then in anger turned his horse round and rode back toward the Shadowed Wood.

"They're on the run!" Nadia shouted. "Let's go after them!"

I knew something that Nadia obviously didn't – the troops of Diabolus are extremely cunning. I'd already seen the army of at least two hundred Doubters hiding in the Shadowed Wood. They went under names like Salvation Doubters, Free Forgiveness Doubters, Resurrection Doubters, Heaven Doubters, Bible Doubters, Miracle Doubters and many more –

and they had All-Except-Me giving them their orders.

Nadia let Choosing go in front, but of course without the army of the King's Son for support, she and her friends would be easy prey.

"Look at their Swords," Talora said breathlessly, as we hurried to keep up. "They're in terrible condition."

I knew that All-Except-Me was being crafty. He was making his troops appear to be retreating in fear to the shelter of the wood, while Nadia and her friends chased after them eagerly with their rusty Swords held high.

Then Won't-Believe gave the signal for the drummer to beat his drum.

Furiously.

Boom and *boom* and *boom* and *boom*.

At this signal, the army of Doubters leapt from their hiding places in the Shadowed Wood with dreadful, terrible cries.

Choosing immediately held up his hands in surrender. He could see that he had been tricked. All around we could hear the cries of Nadia's friends as they fell to the weapons of the Doubters.

I noticed an orange light reflected from the damp tree trunks. I turned round to see Castle Nadia on fire, flames leaping into the night sky.

The drum of the army of Doubters beat louder and louder, the sound filling Nadia's friends with despair. *Boom* and *boom* and *boom* and *boom*. They tried to stop their ears with their fingers to keep out the noise as they fought the mighty army of Diabolus, using their own strength as their only weapon.

CHAPTER 38

All-Except-Me

By the early morning light sifting through the sickly trees, we could see Nadia and her friends lying motionless on the ground where they'd fallen to the Doubters' weapons.

"Zephan, they are all dead," Talora whispered, as tears welled up in her eyes.

But she was wrong. As the sun rose higher, Nadia's friends began to move, standing up slowly and painfully. Nadia stayed where she had fallen in the battle. It was a sorry group that limped and crawled back to Castle Nadia. The army of Doubters had gone, but Nadia's friends said they were terrified they'd be back soon.

That was when we caught sight of the King's Son, standing over Nadia. He lifted her in his arms and carried her tenderly to her fire-blackened castle. Her friends cried out in joy when they saw Nadia was alive, and began to clap. Although we'd not seen him, the King's Son must have been watching over Nadia and her friends all night long.

The King's Son placed Nadia gently on the grass outside her castle door. "Nadia," he said, "you are very precious to me. Did you think you could fight my enemies by yourself?"

Nadia said nothing. In shame she stood up, head hung low, and crept into her castle. In the scorched doorway she paused.

"I cannot answer the King's Son," she told her friends.

"Look at the state of your castle, Nadia," one girl said. "Perhaps the King's Son could restore it for you."

Nadia shook her head sadly. "I'd like him to, but I don't have the courage to ask him."

The castle was still standing, in spite of the devastating fire that one of the unpleasant creatures must have started. Nadia went in and shut and bolted the door that still looked strong enough to resist further attack. And there she stayed, all alone.

Was she comfortable? I doubt it, but she lived in her castle as best she could. As the weeks turned into months, brambles and nettles grew around the walls, thorns climbing higher and higher until they prevented the sunlight from penetrating even the highest windows. It seemed a desolate place now. But some of Nadia's old friends said they thought it a fine castle, and laughed as they passed by.

Conscience had been badly wounded, and spent every day sitting on the castle doorstep alone and forlorn. Understanding crawled into a tunnel under the walls and slowly began to lose his eyesight. Choosing hid under the bushes day and night, afraid the shadow angels were coming back.

Talora and I flew over Castle Nadia from time to time, unseen by Nadia and her friends. Only the secret room of the Spirit was untouched by the decay that had spread throughout the rest of the once- splendid building.

I want to make it clear that we weren't wasting our time while all this was going on. When Max called to the King's Son for help – and he did this every day – the King's Son often sent us to give him a hand, although Max was never able to see us again. I don't know if he guessed we were there, but he always gave thanks to the King's Son for help. He never thanked us personally – which may sound ungrateful, but it's exactly how it should be.

Talora sat with me by Castle Nadia one night after we'd returned from helping Max knock down a newly built shack behind his castle, and she began to cry openly. "Tell me, Zephan, why does Nadia not ask the Holy Spirit to send another message to the King? She did it before the castle was ruined, but now all she and her special friends do is sit nursing their wounds, feeling sorry for themselves."

I had no answer to that.

CHAPTER 39

The Letter

One night there was great panic. All-Except-Me appeared with a troop of shadow angels swarming all over the place, trying to smash Castle Nadia to the ground. Love-God called to Conscience and Choosing to join Nadia and fight boldly to help her resist the attack.

By dawn the skirmish was over. All-Except-Me and his troops had withdrawn, defeated. Even in its sorry state, the army of Doubters had come to realise that while the Holy Spirit lived there, Castle Nadia was secure. Choosing, however, had been severely wounded in the fighting, and for a time I was afraid he would die.

The next morning Love-God stood outside the blackened walls. Nadia and some of her wounded friends came to hear what she had to say. "You must each send another plea to the King for forgiveness. Go boldly to the Holy Spirit and ask for his help in writing your letters. And go now."

This seemed to put fresh heart into everyone, for although Love-God looked young, they obviously respected her.

At the secret room where the Holy Spirit dwelt, the door was slightly open. Nadia knocked and walked into the room hesitatingly, while her friends waited outside the castle in hopeful anticipation. I was sure I could hear their hearts beating loudly with anxiety but, as I said earlier, angels seem to have especially good hearing.

"Is the Holy Spirit still there?" we heard someone call.

"Even if he is, will he take any notice of Nadia?" another friend asked.

It was time to listen through one of the higher open windows. We felt such love for Nadia and Max that we wanted everything to work out well for them – especially if we could help in any way. Brambles had spread thickly even to this height, covering the open window with thorns. But we managed to pull them away without getting too many scratches.

"My treasured Nadia, you have not been here for a long time. What do you want?" We could hear great tenderness and patience in the Holy Spirit's voice.

Nadia must have sensed it too, for she took encouragement and knelt down, hanging her head in shame as she spoke. "You know how badly we have behaved. We have allowed the army of Diabolus to defeat us. We are not able ..."

The Holy Spirit stopped her. "Nadia," he said gently, "I want to hear what *you* have done, not your friends."

"But we've *all* ..." Nadia put her hand to her mouth. "I'm sorry. *I* have behaved badly. *I* have allowed Diabolus and his friends to defeat *me*. *I* cannot get an answer from the King's Son."

"And?" the Holy Spirit asked. "You have not told me yet what it is you want."

"I want the King's Son to forgive me. I've been forgetting what he did for me. Now I want to know him again, but I think I've gone too far away from the love of the Lord God to deserve mercy. I believe *some* people deserve to be forgiven – but not me."

The Holy Spirit shook his head. "Deserve mercy? No one *deserves* mercy, Nadia – not even the most holy person on Earth. Mercy and forgiveness are gifts. I am afraid you have let All-Except-Me whisper in your ear for too long. When he comes again you must destroy him with your Sword.”

“Then please write a letter asking for forgiveness,” Nadia begged. “Surely the King will listen when *you* write to him.”

The Holy Spirit told Nadia to kneel by his side. “First of all you must forget what you heard from All-Except-Me.” He put his arms round her shoulders and held her with such tenderness that Nadia told her friends later it felt as though the whole power of the Lord God flowed through her. “The promises of the King’s Son are for *you*,” the Holy Spirit added.

When she heard this, Nadia began to cry.

“I cannot write for you,” the Holy Spirit explained. “I can provide ink and paper, but you must do the writing yourself. How else could you say it is from you?”

Nadia smiled and wiped her eyes. She said it made her happy to know that she’d found the way to reach the King, with her plea for the Prince to return. But even as she wrote the letter, the sound of Diabolus’ drum started to echo through the castle.

Boom and *boom* and *boom* and *boom*.

Several times Nadia stopped in fear, saying it might be better to go out and fight the enemy rather than to continue writing the letter.

“Nadia, have you not learnt your lesson?” the Holy Spirit asked. “You are not to fight evil in your own strength.”

At last Nadia finished, in spite of the interruptions from outside, and put her pen down.

The Holy Spirit took the letter and sealed it himself. “I will send it at once,” he told her. “You had a hard lesson to learn, Nadia, and you have been very stubborn. The King has allowed your castle to be broken. Take courage now, for the answer will not be long in coming.”

“I’d like to write some letters for my friends,” Nadia said.

"No, Nadia. You can *help* your friends write letters, but the words must be their own. It must be their decision, their will."

Quickly Nadia ran outside to tell her friends the news. Some returned to their castles immediately to take up pen and paper, but a few stayed and said they wanted to see how it all worked out for Nadia before writing anything themselves.

Diabolus kept beating his drum all through the rest of the day, and then into the night while we sat on the grass outside Castle Nadia. In spite of the letters, Nadia and her friends trembled in their beds. The army of Doubters and the companions of Diabolus ran noisily around the castles, singing and shouting that Diabolus was coming to destroy everyone with his sharp and dreadful sword.

In the end it all became too much for us, and I knelt down with Talora and called out to the King's Son. We should have done it much earlier, but that's how it was. The King's Son spoke to us immediately.

"Do not think I enjoy such events as these," he explained, as the drum grew silent at last. "Max and his friends had for a long time been calling out to me to come and receive Nadia as my own. Now you can see why I brought the catapults and the battering ram. It was to make Nadia aware of my existence."

"And it worked," I said, remembering how Nadia had at first been angry, and then pleased to hear the King's Son calling her. "But her new faith didn't last," I added.

"It was not necessary for Nadia or her friends to turn away from me, but they listened to too many other voices, besides mine. And so did two of Max's friends. There has been much sadness in Heaven over this. Zephan and Talora, look over there beyond the hills. Today will be a day of victory that Nadia and everyone with her will remember for the rest of their lives."

CHAPTER 40

Soldiers!

As the sky grew lighter, I could see Castle Max down in the dip still looking weak, although we now knew a greater force than nature kept it secure. I remembered how strong we thought Castle Nadia looked on that first day when we arrived from the planet Eltor, and it depressed me to see that the building was now such a mess. The brambles and nettles had grown even higher and thicker over the last few days, covering most of the burnt and blackened walls.

I flew up to the top of Castle Nadia with Talora and looked towards the Shadowed Wood, and … I wouldn't be surprised if my face went pale at what I saw. "Keep back, Talora!" I warned.

Talora looked across at me in alarm. "What is it?"

"There are hundreds of soldiers out there," I told her. "*Hundreds.*"

Talora's eyes lit up. "Then we must be happy," she said. "Nadia asked for the King's Son to come, and now he's bringing his warrior angels."

"*No, no!*" I said in panic. "The soldiers are shadow angels. They're coming from Shadow Hill and they'll surround us at any moment. What will happen to Nadia now?"

We heard a furious knocking on the castle door. I looked down but didn't recognise the caller.

I said, "It might be a trick. I hope Nadia doesn't open the door."

Before I could do anything, Choosing limped slowly on crutches to a window. He'd been so badly wounded, fighting All-Except-Me and the Doubters, that at the time I thought he might never walk again.

"Who's knocking?" he called down. "Nadia is still asleep."

"Let me in! Let me in!" the frantic plea came from the front of the castle.

"What do you want?" Choosing asked after a long silence.

"I have a message for Nadia. It's from the King."

Choosing hurried downstairs and opened a small sliding panel in the door so he could see the messenger. "Why, I know you," he said. "You're Captain Faith. You are a brave fighter. What message do you bring?"

Choosing opened the door just wide enough for Captain Faith to slip through, then shut it quickly, slamming the heavy bolts back in place. I flew down to the door with Talora, and we put our ears to the small panel Choosing had used to speak to Captain Faith.

"I have a package from the Lord God," we heard Faith say. "Call Nadia, and we can open it together."

I guessed Nadia would take a few minutes to wake up, so we decided to tell Nadia's friends that she'd received a reply. Quickly I flew with Talora to other castles where we could see white flags, passing on the good news.

"Come to Castle Nadia," we said. "Nadia has received an answer to her letter!"

The people hurried from their doorways, shielding their eyes from the bright morning light. I flew with Talora back to Castle Nadia, leaving her friends to make their own way there.

"We're alone!" I said, as we dropped down onto the grass

outside the castle door.

"What do you mean?" Talora asked

"The shadow angels. They've gone. That's why it's so quiet."

It was an easy mistake to make, for I certainly thought Diabolus had called his army away when Captain Faith arrived. I had no idea the shadow angels were so close, hiding and plotting their attack.

Then we saw someone else knocking on the castle door.

"Nadia, open up. It's me, Love-God."

Nadia opened the door and quickly dragged Love-God inside. "I'm so glad to see you," we heard Nadia say. "Captain Faith is here. We're just about to open a package from the King. Come quickly, and we'll open it together."

Talora beckoned to me and we flew to the open window where we had already cleared the brambles away, in time to see the Holy Spirit unfold a long banner from the King's Son. He started to explain its meaning to Nadia, while Love-God, Choosing and Captain Faith listened.

Then we heard the drum again. The forces of Diabolus were back.

Outside the castle, the friends of Nadia had already arrived. They held their heads when they heard the drum, and what had been rejoicing soon turned to despair.

Choosing looked out of the window. "All-Except-Me is down there with his army of Doubters," he shouted to Nadia in panic. "Stay indoors and don't listen to his evil talk."

Sad to say, Nadia was quickly on her feet, dropping the King's banner to the floor as she rushed to the window. We moved to one side, out of view.

"Greetings, Nadia," All-Except-Me called loudly from below.

Nadia stood in the open window. "What do you want?" she

demanded, more than a little anxiously.

"I mean you no harm, Nadia, but you can surely see that your castle and your friends are outnumbered. You have Captain Faith with you. You do not need him. Send Captain Faith, and him alone, to me. Then I will leave you in peace."

Nadia turned to Choosing for advice.

Choosing shook his head. "Captain Faith is one of the King's men," he told her. "If you send him out there you might as well *give* your castle to the Doubters."

Nadia shouted down words to this effect.

"Foolish talk!" All-Except-Me spat angrily.

At that moment a great cheer went up from Nadia's friends outside the castle. From the window of the Holy Spirit's secret room floated a long banner – the message that had just arrived from the Lord God.

The one who comes to me I will certainly not cast out.

Then something extraordinary happened. Somehow, in all the excitement, All-Except-Me had managed to creep unseen through the castle door. Nadia spotted him climbing the stairs, and grabbed hold of his arm. Quickly she picked up the Sword the King's Son had given her earlier. It looked cleaner and sharper now. With a shout she threw All-Except-Me to the floor and using both hands plunged the blade's sharp point through his chest. All-Except-Me screamed as the powerful steel penetrated his body, then Nadia picked him up and threw him through the open window. Fortunately, Talora and I were able to duck as the lifeless body hurtled past. It crashed to the ground with a sound of breaking bones, and Nadia's friends cheered again.

"I understand it now," Nadia said in excitement. "*The one who comes to me I will certainly not cast out.* It's a message for me from the King's Son. I never understood it properly before.

It's not just for good people – the promise is for *me*, in spite of me being so bad!"

When Won't-Believe and the army of Doubters realised what had happened, and heard Nadia shouting out the words on the banner, they turned away in rage. I could understand why. The Sword had killed All-Except-Me, and now the words on the banner were piercing them. The Holy Book was indeed the sharpest weapon.

Just as I was thinking that the army of Doubters intended to leave Castle Nadia in peace, Won't-Believe suddenly turned round. "Sound the attack!" he screamed. "Sound the attack! The castle will perish!"

At his command, the army of Doubters rushed forward. The sight of the army and the sound of the beating drum made Nadia and her friends nervous. Yet, as they looked at the promise on the banner, we could feel their trust in the Lord God growing stronger.

"Take the castle," Won't-Believe ordered the shadow angels. "Nadia will be ours – if we can get inside!"

With Won't-Believe leading them, the Doubters encircled Castle Nadia and prepared to storm the door.

Then the voice of Diabolus came clearly from the direction of Shadow Hill. Nadia and her friends would not have been able to hear him, but shadow angels could, and so could we as the Lord God's angels.

"Come back to the cover of the wood," Diabolus ordered his troops. "You can hide there until these people forget about the Lord G ... the Lord G ... the King again. It will be easy to take the castle when Nadia and her friends have forgotten the words on the banner."

Won't-Believe sounded impatient. "Victory must be ours *today!*" he shouted. "Why, by this time tomorrow the King's

Son may be here. There is no time to lose!"

Diabolus, however, seemed unable to make up his mind. Sometimes he called out one plan, and sometimes another. While this was going on, Nadia and her friends were reading their Holy Books, sharpening their Swords, putting on their armour and gaining fresh strength to resist the attack.

"Draw them away from the castle," Diabolus shouted. He had left Shadow Hill now, and was coming closer on horseback. "When they split up, you can destroy them one at a time."

"They will not be so stupid as to fight us again in their own strength," Won't-Believe told the army of Doubters impatiently, ignoring his orders. "To war, I say, and the victory will be ours this very hour!"

I hovered with Talora above the castle. For the moment Diabolus had his way, and the army withdrew.

"Where's the King's Son?" I asked Talora. "He promised to help." I'm not sure if I felt impatient at the time or not. You have to bear in mind we were caught up in something terrible.

Talora put a finger to her lips. "Do not doubt the King's Son," she said. "I can sense his love, even though there is so much evil below."

Captain Faith called Nadia and her friends together. "Don't be afraid," he shouted confidently. "You have seen the promise from the King's Son on the banner. Read it again."

Led by Nadia, her friends read the words aloud. "*The one who comes to me I will certainly not cast out.*" They repeated the promise over and over.

"These words are for *you*," Captain Faith told them. "All-Except-Me is dead, and you no longer have to listen to his false messages of doubt."

"But where *is* the King's Son?" Nadia asked. "Please tell us."

Captain Faith smiled. "Soon he will be outside this castle to do battle with the army of Diabolus. Hurry to your castles and gather every trumpet you can find, and then come back here and blow them loudly, ready to receive the Son of the Lord God!"

Within a few minutes Nadia and her friends began to blow long and loud on their trumpets outside Castle Nadia. At first the trumpets sounded rather tuneless, but after a few minutes the music became harmonious, so that it seemed like a chorus of praise rising to the rescuer who was on his way.

"What is the meaning of this noise?" Diabolus shouted to Won't-Believe.

"They seem to think, sir, that they are about to be rescued," Won't-Believe told him, trying to conceal his trembling limbs.

Diabolus spat on the ground. "We must hold back from the attack. I have no wish to be defeated."

"We *cannot* be defeated," Won't-Believe said firmly.

Diabolus turned away angrily. Clearly he didn't want his soldiers to see fear of the Lord God in his eyes.

CHAPTER 41

Swords and Shields

There was great excitement at Castle Nadia. Nadia and her friends were now well armed, having cleaned and sharpened their Swords to prepare themselves for this great battle.

"The Sword of the Prince and the Shield of Faith!" Nadia called, but not very loudly.

Everyone took up the cry, louder and louder, until the sound echoed off the neighbouring castles. *"The Sword of the Prince and the Shield of Faith!"*

Diabolus lost his temper. With a mighty roar he ordered his army to attack. Nadia and her friends let fly at his army with weapons the King's Son had given them.

"The Sword of the Prince and the Shield of Faith!" they shouted again.

So loud was the battle cry that the forces of Diabolus shrank back.

"The Prince is close at hand!" Captain Faith called loudly

Thinking this was merely a trick, the troops of Diabolus hurled themselves once more at Castle Nadia. Each time, the weapons of the Prince drove them back. Then Nadia let out a great shout.

"The Prince is coming! The King's Son is coming!"

With flags and banners flying, trumpets sounding, and the

feet of his men and horses scarcely touching the ground, the Son of the Lord God rode up the hill from the valley.

"Emmanuel, Emmanuel!" the people cried.

"God with us! God with us!" echoed from around the castle walls.

Diabolus looked terrified. In front of him he could see Nadia and her friends – well armed with the King's weapons. Behind him was the angel army of the Lord God, approaching fast.

Leaving his army to fight their way out, Diabolus dug his spurs into his horse and raced away to the shelter of the Shadowed Wood.

We watched as the mighty warrior angels of Heaven set on the army of Doubters. Before long they all lay dead on the ground, cold and silent like stones along a beach. Led by Nadia, her friends ran to meet the Son of God. He held up his hand to bless them.

"Peace," he said loudly, so that everyone could hear his words of welcome. "You cannot understand how pleased I am to be with you this day. Over and over I will forgive all the wrong things you do. Let us talk together, for I have many plans for you."

Talora looked at me. Nadia and her friends certainly seemed at peace again. The white flag of the Spirit flew clean and high on top of Castle Nadia, and I remember thinking how different it was from the old homemade flag Nadia had copied from one that belonged to someone in her family.

Now that the shadow angels had gone we no longer felt afraid. The King's Son was in charge. Nadia had allowed herself to be broken, before realising that the King's Son would not come and go whenever it pleased her for him to do so. Now, at last, Nadia knew how much she loved and needed the Prince –

and how much he loved and needed her.

We walked past Castle Max to two castles we'd not noticed before.

"Sit down, Zephan," Talora said. "I feel strangely sleepy."

As we lay back against a large, smooth rock, the landscape before us seemed to break into different shapes.

"We're going back to the planet Eltor," I said. "Our adventure is over. See, everything is changing."

Talora shook her head. "No, look at the sky. It's still blue."

Then something amazing happened. Angels were everywhere. I don't just mean warrior angels. I mean ordinary angels like me, like Talora. These angels must have been here all along, but the King's Son had hidden them from our sight. I laughed aloud to think that I'd imagined we were alone. But we'd come through the test, so we would be able to do the Lord God's work here on Earth. Of course, I'd miss the planet Eltor – especially the little giskos – but working here would be extra special.

Something else looked different too. The castles had gone – and so had the white flags – and we saw people walking and driving around in the sort of world you know so well, the world as it really is.

The voice of the Lord God floated softly over the hill. "*Talora and Zephan, there are many people here who do not fly my flag. They have not invited me in. If you are to stay and help me, would you rather see them with their castles or just as people?*"

"With their castles," Talora and I said together. I wasn't sure we were ready for too many changes, and with castles we'd learnt where to find problems. I mean, how would we know what people were thinking if we didn't see what was going in their lives without their thoughts and troubles looking like

Great-Hopes, Good-Deeds and Self-Righteous – and even Love-God?

"And will you work for me even though you know the dangers?"

"We love you," I said, and it wasn't bravado. Certainly there was danger, great danger. The battles might be tough, but we knew we were on the winning side. "We will serve you on Earth while there is work to be done here," I added.

Again the landscape changed, but the sky was still bright blue. Small castles rose from the ground. We recognised Castle Nadia and Castle Max in the distance, with their white flags flying high. Castle Max might appear weak, but the Lord God was looking after it, and you can't ask for more than that.

I rubbed my eyes in surprise to see how clean Castle Nadia looked. The blackened walls were already washed clean and repaired. It felt good to think we'd be seeing a lot more of Max and Nadia. What was less pleasant was to see how many castles had no flags. Some had brambles and nettles covering the walls and windows, others looked so cheerless. The two closest castles had the names Castle James and Castle Sophie over their doors. I remembered Max and his friends mentioning James and Sophie in their prayers.

I blinked as Good-Deeds strode past, making for Castle James. I noticed that the castle had no white flag on top. Over there I was sure I could see Self-Pleasing sneering outside Castle Sophie. And that looked like All-Except-Me carrying planks of wood on his shoulder. But surely he was dead. Anyway, it definitely looked like him.

From the valley came the sound of horses galloping. With the King's Son as their leader, the five captains rode to the door of Castle James.

The first was Captain Trust, carrying his blood red banner

with the picture of the Lamb. Then came Captain Good-Hope, with his blue banner showing the three golden anchors. The third was Captain Love. His banner had the picture of young people being held securely by the King's Son.

Captain Innocent was the fourth. His white banner unfurled slowly in the breeze to show the picture of three golden doves. Captain Patience came last. You may remember that his banner showed tears shed by the King's Son as he waited and cried for the people he loved to turn to him.

The King's Son signalled to us to join him.

Talora jumped to her feet and spread her wings. "Come on, Zephan," she said, giving me a friendly slap on the back, "we can't sit here all day. There's work to be done."

EPILOGUE

Excuse me for asking, but do you think you could be like Nadia at the start of this story, with a homemade flag on your castle, one copied from someone in your family? Maybe this is the first time you've even thought about it. Do you want a genuine flag? Or maybe you've never really thought about God before. The words on the banner – *The one who comes to me I will certainly not cast out* – are just one of many promises from Jesus. You can find this one in John 6:37. The translation here is from the New American Standard Bible. Read the words for yourself in your own Bible and remember them carefully. They are a great defence against the whispers of All-Except-Me.

John Bunyan ends *The Holy War* with the King's Son talking to Mansoul. I have taken three sections of this ending, because they seem to round off this allegory so well – in spite of the very old fashioned wording which is from the original.

What sort of "castle" are you? Instead of *Mansoul*, put your own name in the word below, because in a way each of us *is* Mansoul.

"You, my Mansoul, and the beloved of mine heart, many and great are the privileges that I have bestowed upon you; I have singled you out from others, and have chosen you to myself, not for your worthiness, but for mine own sake. I have also redeemed you, not only from the dread of my Father's law, but from the hand of Diabolus. This I have done because I loved you, and because I have set my heart upon you to do you good."

"O my Mansoul, I have lived, I have died, I live, and will die no more for thee. I live, that thou mayest not die. Because I live, thou shalt live also. I reconciled thee to my Father by the blood of my cross; and being reconciled, thou shalt live through me. I will pray for thee; I will fight for thee; I will yet do thee good."

"Remember, therefore, O my Mansoul, that thou art beloved of me: as I have, therefore, taught thee to watch, to fight, to pray, and to make war against my foes; so now I command thee to believe that my love is constant to thee. O my Mansoul, how have I set my heart, my love upon thee!"

Chris Wright

Chris Wright's website is www.rocky-island.com, and you can contact him from a link on there if you like.

AGATHOS,
THE ROCKY ISLAND,
AND OTHER STORIES
Chris Wright

ISBN 978-0-9525956-8-7
White Tree Publishing

Once upon a time there were two favorite books for Sunday reading: *Parables From Nature* and *Agathos and The Rocky Island.*

These books contained all sorts of short stories, usually with a hidden meaning. In this illustrated book there is a selection of the very best of these stories, carefully retold to preserve the feel of the originals, coupled with ease of reading and understanding for today's readers.

Discover the king who sent his servants to trade in a foreign city; the butterfly who thought her eggs would hatch into baby butterflies; and the two boys who decided to explore the forbidden land beyond the castle boundary. The spider that kept being blown in the wind; the soldier who had to fight a dragon; the four children who had to find their way through a dark and dangerous forest. These are just six of the nine stories in this collection. Oh, and there's also one about a rocky island!

This is a book for a young person to read alone; a family or parent to read aloud; Sunday school teachers to read to the class; and even for grownups who want to dip into the fascinating stories of the past all by themselves. Can you discover the hidden meanings? You don't have to wait until Sunday before starting!

5.5 x 8.5 inches 148 pages £5.95
Available from major internet stores

MARY JONES
AND HER BIBLE
AN ADVENTURE BOOK
(ENDORSED BY BIBLE SOCIETY)
Chris Wright

ISBN: 978-0-9525956-2-5
White Tree Publishing

Take part in Mary Jones' adventure! Mary Jones saved for six years to buy a Bible of her own – and after walking 26 miles (over 40km) to get it, she discovered there were none for sale!

Mary made her walk alone, barefoot over a mountain pass and through deep valleys in Wales in 1800, at the age of 15. You can travel with her today in this book as you follow the clues and solve the puzzles. You, too, will get to Bala where Mary travelled, and if you're really quick you may be able to "buy" a Bible just like Mary's!

The true story of Mary Jones and her Bible has captured the imagination for more than 200 years. For this book, Chris Wright has delved deep into the records and come up with the latest facts that are known about Mary.

Packed with puzzles, photographs of real places, and all sorts of fascinating information. If a puzzle is too difficult, or you just don't like puzzles at all, you can turn the page and keep reading. Solving puzzles is part of the fun, but the story is still there to read and enjoy whether you have a go at the puzzles or not. Can you discover the story of Mary Jones?

5.5 x 8.5 inches 158 pages £6.95
Available from bookshops
and major internet stores

PILGRIM'S PROGRESS
AN ADVENTURE BOOK

Chris Wright

ISBN: 978-0-9525956-6-3
White Tree Publishing

Travel with young Christian as he sets out on a difficult and perilous journey to find the King. Solve the puzzles and riddles along the way, and help Christian reach the Celestial City. Then travel with his friend Christiana. She has four young brothers who can sometimes be a bit of a problem.

Be warned, you will meet giants and lions – and even dragons! There are people who don't want Christian and Christiana to reach the city of the King and his Son. But not everyone is an enemy. There are plenty of friendly people. It's just a matter of finding them.

Are you prepared to help? Are you sure? The journey can be very dangerous! As with our book *Mary Jones and Her Bible*, you can enjoy the story even if you don't want to try the puzzles.

This is a simplified and abridged version of *Pilgrim's Progress – Special Edition*, containing illustrations and a mix of puzzles. The suggested reading age is up to perhaps ten. Older readers will find the same story told in much greater detail in *Pilgrim's Progress — Special Edition*.

5.5 x 8.5 inches 174 pages £6.95
Available from major internet stores

PILGRIM'S PROGRESS
SPECIAL EDITION
Chris Wright

ISBN: 978-0-9525956-7-0
White Tree Publishing

This book for all ages is a great choice for young readers, as well as for families, Sunday school teachers, and anyone who wants to read John Bunyan's *Pilgrim's Progress* in a clear form.

All the old favourites are here: Christian, Christiana, the Wicket Gate, Interpreter, Hill Difficulty with the lions, the four sisters at the House Beautiful, Vanity Fair, Giant Despair, Faithful and Talkative – and, of course, Greatheart. The list is almost endless.

The first part of the story is told by Christian himself, as he leaves the City of Destruction to reach the Celestial City, and becomes trapped in the Slough of Despond near the Wicket Gate. On his journey he will encounter lions, giants, and a creature called the Destroyer.

Christiana follows along later, and tells her own story in the second part. Not only does Christiana have to cope with her four young brothers, she worries whether her clothes are good enough for meeting the King. Will she find the dangers in Vanity Fair that Christian found? Will she be caught by Giant Despair and imprisoned in Doubting Castle? What about the dragon with seven heads?

It's a dangerous journey, but Christian and Christiana both know that the King's Son is with them, helping them through the most difficult parts until they reach the Land of Beulah, and see the Celestial City on the other side of the Dark River. This is a story you will remember for ever, and it's about a journey you can make for yourself.

5.5 x 8.5 inches 278 pages £8.95
Available from major internet stores

9 780952 595694